SNOW KISSES FOR MY OMEGA

HOBSON HILLS OMEGAS: BOOK TWO

C.W. GRAY

*H*arper Wilson steadily fed the piece of cedar through the wood planer, leveling it out. Soon enough, he'd moved on to cutting and shaping the wood for the bookcase. Snow fell outside the windows, a silent and beautiful contrast to the warmth of the woodshop. The hum of the planer and the smell of cedar soothed, strengthened, and stabilized him.

His workshop was a place of peace. Stacks of wood were separated into piles, waiting on him to decide what new project he wanted to work on. Each of his tools and equipment had a purpose and a place. It was *his* space, which is why his alpha dad stood out so much. The large man was sprawled in a chair a few feet away, resting his feet.

"When are you going to Florida to get that boy?" Marco Wilson was a big, broad-shouldered alpha. He looked rough around the edges, but the man was one of the kindest people Harper knew.

"Dad, I can't just go kidnap him," Harper said. "He

keeps putting me off about meeting in person." He shrugged, trying to appear nonchalant. "Maybe he just wants to stay friends."

Marco snorted. "Bullshit. You two talk to each other every single night. That doesn't say friends to me."

"I don't know, Dad. I don't know what to do."

"Go visit him and see him in person. Then bring him home, so we can meet him."

"You just want another kid to love on," Harper teased.

"Maybe," Marco said with a grin. "Your papa wants to have another baby before we get too old."

"Aren't you already too old," Harper said, setting his clean board down and picking up another rough piece.

"Thanks, son," Marco said wryly. "Anyway, I've never seen you smile so damn much over someone. This man is special."

"He is," Harper agreed.

Greyson Bishop was a joy to know. He was handsome and honey colored. He had light brown hair streaked with a warm blond, complimenting his golden-brown skin and eyes. To Harper, Grey was pure sunshine.

"That's what I'm talking about," Marco said, throwing his hands up. "That tone of voice, that look in your eyes. I know love when I see it, Harper."

"I'm not saying I don't love him," Harper said. "I'm saying I don't think he loves me. It doesn't mean I'm not going after him. It just means it may take some time."

"Fine," Marco said, sighing. "I guess you're young, so I shouldn't push you to settle down so soon."

"Oh, I'm ready to settle down," Harper said.

He'd been ready since he was sixteen. All he'd ever wanted was a warm, cozy home and a loyal omega that loved him. Babies would be great, but they weren't a requirement. Love and acceptance were.

"I just have to woo my omega a bit first. There's no rush." Harper's phone chimed, and he paused to look at the screen. "Fuck, not again."

"What's wrong?"

"Andrew has been posting disgusting comments on my website as reviews. I blocked him twice now, but he just creates a new account."

"You two broke up over two years ago, didn't you?"

"Yes, and we only dated for two months. He's a whacko, Dad."

"Should we talk to someone about it? Maybe one of the Bensons or the police?"

"I don't want to drudge up old memories. I'll just block him again."

After cutting another board, he set it aside and walked to one of his worktables. His most recent batch of wooden ornaments were dry and ready to pack up.

Marco peeked over his shoulder. "Annie will love those. They've been selling like hotcakes in the store. Do you have more wreathes too? With Christmas coming up, she wants a bunch to set back. When they start going, they go fast."

"I do. I have fifty ornaments to bring her and about ten bowls, tons of decorated wooden utensils, and twenty-two wreathes. I'll make more this weekend. I have a few large projects to finish."

"She'll be a happy woman. You taking a turn at the Christmas tree farm this weekend? If you don't have time, I'll do a shift."

"I should be good for it."

Marco clapped him on the back. "I'll bring your goods in to Annie on the way home. I need to shovel the damn snow from the walk before your papa murders me."

Harper smiled. His dad hated shoveling snow. He was fine when he was hip deep in the stuff, tending to the cattle, but when it came to simply shoveling it, he became a big whiney baby. "Now I see why you really came over. Yes, Dad, I will shovel the walks tomorrow morning. Tell Papa not to worry about it."

"You're a good boy, Harper," Marco said, his smile wide, showing off the gap between his two front teeth that every Wilson inherited from Grammy. "Your brother is going to be working at Zac's auto shop after school for a while. He's convinced he wants to be a mechanic."

"He does good work on my truck," Harper said. "It's his kind of thing."

Marco smiled proudly. "Well, help me load up and I'll get out of your hair."

Harper boxed up the ornaments and added them to the stack of boxes near the door, then helped his dad load them in the back of his truck.

Marco grabbed him and hugged him tightly. "Say hi to your omega for me, okay?"

Harper watched him drive off and turned back to his home. When he'd turned eighteen and told his dad and papa that he was going to work on selling his furniture and crafts, they'd gifted him twenty acres in place of college tuition. It was up the mountain, isolated, and surrounded by forest. The acreage itself was heavily wooded but had a few acres of clear space. It had taken months, but Gramps, Marco, and him had built the cabin by hand.

It was a two story with four bedrooms, one set up as an office, and two bathrooms on the second floor. The first floor was an open plan containing a large kitchen with an attached mudroom, a living room with a large stone fireplace, and another bathroom. To finish it off, they'd added a wrap-around porch and a detached garage. Harper loved it.

The only thing missing was his omega.

Shaking his head, he turned away and headed toward the back. His workshop was attached to a large barn. Harper crunched through the snow and opened the big barn doors, slipping in. He closed the cold back out, then grabbed the hayfork and loaded fresh hay into the two occupied stalls.

Dumpling was a fuzzy, brown miniature Shetland pony. His cream-colored hair needed a brushing, so Harper grabbed the brush and got to work. Dumpling didn't care. His nose was buried in his hay. Boon, his black and white miniature Shetland, poked his nose over to investigate.

"I'll get to you, Boonie-boy," Harper said, laughing.

After grooming and pampering his boys, Harper

went to a small corner of the barn. He had a chicken coop set up in the warmth. They had an outdoor run, but the girls really didn't like the snow. He collected eight eggs, washing them and setting them aside. He only had ten hens and a rooster, but they produced plenty of eggs. The customers loved the blue and green eggs his girls laid. He'd take a few dozen down to the store to sell tomorrow on his way to shovel his papa's walks.

Back in his workshop, he looked at the half-finished sled in the corner. He needed to get to work if he wanted to have it completed in two weeks. His phone rang from his back pocket, and he checked the number. Andrew, yuck. He pushed ignore and got back to work.

LATER THAT NIGHT, Harper sat in the kitchen with his laptop. Grey's sweet face popped up on the screen, his smile as silly and joyous as usual. Harper's sunshine was adorable.

"Hey," he said.

"Hi, Harper," Grey said. "How's business going?"

"The website is perfect," he said. "I've already sold about a third of my stockpiled furniture, and I have contracted projects scheduled for the next several months."

"Awesome! I knew people would love your stuff. I seriously love those bookshelves you added with the vines carved on the side. Your work is amazing. Is your family doing okay?"

"They're fine. Janelle dropped off another fern for me to try not to kill, and Uncle Barry keeps nagging Zoe about settling down. Same old, same old."

"What does your family's store do for Christmas? I can't believe you all hosted a whole Halloween party." Maybe Harper was wrong, but Grey's golden-brown eyes seemed to be full of longing.

"We have the Christmas tree farm up and going. We'll host ice skating parties for the next few months, and the town will have a winter festival in a couple of weeks. The store gets super busy too. People are Christmas shopping, so my smaller crafts are going fast. The chair and bedframe sales have gone up too."

"That sounds like so much fun," Grey said, hints of wistfulness in his voice.

"Tell me about your favorite Christmas," Harper said. He loved to hear about Grey as a kid.

"Oh my god," Grey said, laughing. "So one year, Rue and I were so horrible. We fought all the time, and my parents were probably about to sell us to a circus or something. A few weeks before Christmas, they kicked us out and made us go play with one of our neighbor's kids. The boy was a jerk though. He was an alpha and thought omegas should wait on him hand and foot. Of course, I didn't, so he got really mad and called me names. Rue was a year younger than me, and three years younger than the asshole, but he got in the kid's face and made him shut up. The neighbor wasn't happy, but when we got home, we were fine, no more arguing. My parents were so happy, they went all out that year with a huge tree, lots of decorations, and cookies. Christmas eve night, Rue snuck in my room. We read comics and talked all night. It was awesome."

"I have to admit, siblings can be both a pain and a joy," Harper said with a laugh. "I wonder if Dad or Papa ever wanted to sell us to a circus."

"Surely not," Grey said, smiling. "You're always so patient. Your brother and sister probably adore you."

"Hmm, I'll have to remind them that they should, indeed, adore me." Harper watched Grey laugh, eyes sparkling. Oh, his omega was so beautiful.

CHAPTER 2

"This is stunning, Grey," Harper said, flipping through the baby book Grey had mailed him a few days ago. The handsome alpha grinned, the gap between his front teeth absolutely charming. "I don't know why you won't try to publish this. I'm lending it to my cousin, just so you know. Elijah announced he was pregnant right before Thanksgiving."

"I hope he'll like it," Grey said, glad the camera on his computer only ever showed him from the neck up. His big pregnant belly would have given him away a long time ago. "I remember you said he got married just a few weeks before then. Are they happy about the baby, since it happened so quickly?" He didn't know why he asked, but he wanted to hear about an alpha who actually cared about his omega. One who wanted a baby.

"Oh yeah." Harper said. "Carter is ecstatic."

Of course he is, Grey thought. Maybe Grey was the only one that ended up with an alpha boyfriend who didn't want kids. The asshole had dumped him seconds after Grey showed him the pregnancy test.

"I wish you could have made it for Thanksgiving. When are you going to visit, Grey?" Harper asked, eyes focused on him like a laser. "I could come down there."

"Oh," Grey said, thinking fast. "You wouldn't like it here with all the alligators and tourists."

Harper's deep laugh made Grey shiver. "You said you wanted to get out of Florida. Come visit me. I know you work from home, and I can buy your ticket if that's the problem. We could even invite Abuela. I'd love to meet her."

"Who visits Maine in the winter?"

"Well, it's really cold right now, but the snow is beautiful. You'd like it, and I have plenty of space."

If he had met Harper nine or ten months ago, Grey would already be moved to Maine. He was absolutely crazy about the woodworker. He was kind, gentle, intelligent, and so damn hot. The whole package. But no, instead of meeting Harper, he'd met Ted.

Grey wasn't sure if Harper would even talk to him if he knew Grey was eight months pregnant with another alpha's child. "Maybe... Maybe in few months," he said, putting the handsome alpha off again. In a few months, he'd have a baby. He'd have to come clean to Harper, and then he'd lose him.

"Hey, Fatty!" his roommate's voice called from outside his door. Oh fuck!

"Shit, I have to go, Harper. Talk to you later."

"But, Grey..."

Grey hurriedly closed the video call and jumped out

of his seat. Dorian forced open the door, popping the lock. Again.

"I'm not fat. I'm pregnant." Grey really wished Dorian had never moved in. The last five months had been miserable.

"That baby ain't sitting in your ass, Fatty," he said. "You need to pack your shit and get out by the end of the week."

"What? I have a lease for another three months. I've lived here since starting college. I don't understand." Grey felt like the walls were pushing in, and panic welled, closing his throat.

"Landlord doesn't want a whore omega on his property. You're lucky I talked him into a week. He wanted you out tonight." Dorian roughly pushed Grey's head into the wall, and he heard his nose crunch. He whimpered in pain but kept his eyes on the floor. "You better thank me, Fatty. Start thinking about what you're gonna give me, omega whore."

Tears welled in his eyes. "I'm not a whore. I've only ever slept with two guys my whole life. I'm pregnant. It happens all the time."

"Don't care, Fatty. Just make sure you pay me and get your shit out by Friday." Dorian left, letting the door bang shut behind him.

Grey held his nose and sat on the bed, finally letting himself cry. He hated his life. *I hate myself,* he thought as he shook with his sobs. Six years ago, he was a happy seventeen-year-old. Then his parents and little brother died, leaving him alone. Nothing had gone right in his life since that day. So often, he fought the desire to follow them, to be with them again.

Minutes or hours later, his sobs slowed. His nose throbbed, but it had stopped bleeding. He wiped his face and took a few deep breaths. Looking down, he cupped his huge belly. "It's okay, baby. You're not alone, and I'll take care of us, okay? It might get hard, but I'm here for you, and I love you."

He had to be strong. He wiped his nose on his sleeve and spied the bag of doughnuts he'd left on his desk for dinner. He always ate dinner after talking with Harper. His appetite was always really good after seeing his alpha. He made Grey feel safe and special.

"Come on, baby, let's sing the doughnut song and have dinner." He grabbed the bag and set it on the bed. "Doughnut, doughnut, doughnut," he sang to his belly, swaying back and forth. "This baby loves doughnuts. They're so yummy, so we'll stuff them in my tummy."

Opening the bag, he devoured every last doughnut, then sat again, powder all over his face. Tamales sounded good now, even if they weren't Abuela's. Oh man, what he'd give for her cooking. Grey shook his head, trying to avoid those thoughts. He didn't like to leave his room for too long, so more food was out. Ever since Dorian moved in, some of his things had gone missing. He'd already lost two laptops.

Grey cleaned his face off and looked around his room. He had to think about packing all his things. He had tons of books and his collection of Pop! figures. He was going to have to be an adult now. He was twenty-three. It was time.

"I don't want to move, baby," he said, patting his belly. "Change sucks, and I know these four walls." He hugged his pillow, pressing it against his hot face. "At least we have some money put away, baby boy. I've been saving since I started at Delwick's last year. Maybe we can rent a house with a yard. Hmm, now I wish I had adopted a dog like we wanted. Babies need puppies," he said, then sighed. "What am I saying? I can't even take care of myself and you, let alone a dog."

His ringtone, Bebe Rexha's "I'm a Mess," echoed through the room. Grey recognized the number unfortunately. He put it on speaker phone and flopped back onto his bed. "Hello?"

"Mi corazón, you haven't called me in days." Ines Torres was his favorite person in the whole world, but she was a nosy Catholic. "I haven't seen your sweet face in almost a year. What's wrong?"

"Abuela," Grey said, "nothing's wrong. I'm the same as I was last week."

"Then why won't you come for a visit? Miami isn't that far."

"Uh, my scooter broke down," he lied. "I'm getting it fixed, but it'll be another month." He looked pointedly at his belly. Baby boy would be coming soon.

"Every time I come to visit you, you're not there," she said, and hummed for a moment. "I'm getting very tired of Miami," Abuela said. "The latest neighbor es estúpido. I'm thinking of moving to you. I miss my sweet boy."

"No," Grey yelled, sitting up straight. On one hand, he would love to have her with him always. On the other hand, she'd see his big belly and hate him. "Uh, I mean, that's not a good idea right now. Maybe in a few months?" How would he explain the mystery baby then? He was so stupid.

"You don't want your abuela nearby? You want to go canoodling with your alpha."

"Canoodling, Abuela? Really?" He fought his smile. Ines always made him laugh. His smile slowly disappeared. He couldn't lose her. "I don't have an alpha now. We broke up months ago."

"Ted is gone? Good riddance. He wasn't good enough for you. What about this Harper you talk about all the time?"

"He's not my alpha," Grey said, blushing. "We're just friends."

"You glow when you talk about him, mi corazón," she said, voice soft. "I know this even over the phone."

"He lives in Maine, Abuela. That's too far away for a relationship." His belly was too full of a baby for a relationship too.

"Maine? Don't they have moose there? What about those cats. The kind you like."

"Maine Coons?"

"Yes, those."

"Uh, I don't know if they come from Maine," Grey said. "Australian Shepherds don't come from Australia."

"Look it up, querido," Abuela said. "You should know about the state of your alpha. I'll google it."

"Abuela, he wouldn't want me," Grey said, completely exasperated.

"Why not? You're a good boy," she said. Oh, she wouldn't think so if she knew he was pregnant.

"He's really talented, handsome, intelligent… I could go on and on, but the point is, he's out of my league."

"Estúpido!" Sometimes Grey thought that was her favorite word. "Now, we should visit Maine. I'll ask Lisa from across the street about the snow. She lived in Michigan, you know."

Grey just sighed and let her ramble on. He wished he could go to Maine. He wished for a lot of things though.

After a long conversation with Abuela, some quality time with a new romance novel, and a heating pad for his nose, Grey finally made it to bed. He rolled into a blanket burrito and tried to let the world go.

He didn't notice his laptop was still open or that his video call was still streaming.

CHAPTER 3

*H*arper finished shoveling the front walk, then stretched his back and shoulders. He walked around to the back door and stored the shovel and his wet boots in the mudroom. His parents had a large farm house near the family store, Farm Fresh, but the walks weren't covered, so the snow piled up.

A large pot sat on the stove, and Harper's omega papa was putting together a stew to simmer all day. Fresh bread baked in the oven, filling the large room with a delicious smell.

Bennett Wilson nodded toward a stool. "Park it, sweetie."

Harper sat, nibbling his lip and struggling to think of the words he needed. His papa just waited, patiently cutting vegetables. "I accidently eavesdropped on Grey last night. He left the call on without realizing it."

"Uh oh," Bennett said. "What did you find out?"

"A lot of things," Harper said. "His roommate is an

asshole, he eats doughnuts for dinner, and he likes to sing about his food."

"I don't like the sound of that," Papa said. "Well, except for him singing about his food. That's cute."

"I also found out his last alpha dumped him, and he's pregnant."

Bennett stared at him, mouth hanging open. "Why didn't you start with that? Wait. You're saying he's pregnant, but his roommate was being mean? That son of a bitch!"

"He's getting kicked out of his house too. He has to leave by Friday."

"Hmm," Bennett said, turning back to his cutting board.

"He doesn't have an alpha, and he's really, really pregnant," Harper said. "I can't believe he didn't tell me. I wouldn't judge him, and I wouldn't have cared." Harper had replayed every word he'd heard last night over and over. Why hadn't Grey trusted him?

Bennett paused from cutting carrots for his stew. "Sweetie, I know that and you know that, but Grey has only known you for a few months. I imagine he's already worried and self-conscious. If he likes you half as much as you like him, then he'll be paranoid and overthink everything." He narrowed his eyes. "Like you're doing."

"Good point," he acknowledged. "I bought a ticket to Florida."

Bennett hid his smile and started cutting the potatoes. "I figured you would. Are you bringing him back?"

"That's my plan. Then, I'll need to get him in to see a doctor, get a nursery ready, and get a dog and a Maine Coon cat. The list goes on and on. Having a baby is a big deal, Papa."

"It certainly is," he agreed. "You do know that it's not your baby, right?"

"Of course it's my baby," Harper said, affronted. "Ted, his old alpha, was a damn idiot. I'm not."

"You're only twenty-two, Harper. Are you sure you want to be a dad? It's a lot of work."

"Ready or not, it's happening. I want Grey. I've talked to him for months, and I know that there's no one else for me. You know how hard it is for me, Papa, but I'm certain. He's my sunshine."

"How does he feel about you?"

"I think he cares about me, but he said I was out of his league, which is just plain wrong." The thought of Grey not knowing how special he was hurt Harper. The man was gentle, sweet, silly, and oh so sexy.

"From what you've told me about him, I think he does have some personal issues to work through. You're going to need to be patient, sweetie. Bring him home and let us love on him some. Give him time to settle in," Bennett said, dumping the chopped vegetables into the pot.

"I will," he said.

Bennett walked around the kitchen island and wrapped his arms around Harper. His papa was definitely a hugger, but Harper didn't mind. He loved his softness and warmth. The world could be a hard and cold place.

"I'm happy for you, sweetie. I know you struggle with relationships, but that's not your fault. Some people just can't appreciate those who don't fit some weird socially acceptable norm. You are perfect just like you are."

"Justin didn't think so," Harper said, then scowled. His first boyfriend had no place in this moment.

"Justin was an idiot," Bennett said. "Just like this Ted guy."

Harper grinned. "Good point." He rested his head on his hand. "Grey knows I'm a demi. He looked stuff up and asked questions. He didn't try to tell me how I *should* be, just accepted it."

Bennett grinned. "Well, now."

"We've talked a lot. I told him about Justin and Andrew. He told me about his parents and little brother dying, how he was so alone and wanted to die too."

"What?" Bennett set his knife down again. "His family died? That poor boy."

"He was only seventeen and was on a trip for school. When he got home, he had to identify the bodies. They were in a car accident."

"Oh my god!"

"Since he was close to being eighteen, they granted him adulthood, or something like that. He didn't want to stay in the house though."

"Of course not. It was probably full of memories."

"So he rented a room from an older woman, Ines Torres. She became his abuela and saved him. It was bad, Papa, the way he felt then. All alone."

"We really need to love on your man, sweetie." Bennett looked like he wanted to hunt Grey down right then and hug him until he couldn't take it anymore.

"Now, she doesn't know about him being pregnant either. He's all alone again, and I can't stand it."

"He won't be for long," Bennett said. "I'll put Shawn on the task of readying one of your spare rooms. I'll talk to Dr. Richards in town and make an appointment for Grey. Gramps will find a place for Ines. Do you think she'll come with?"

"If half of what he told me about her is true, she will," Harper said. "Thanks, Papa."

"Now, for the most important question of all. Why on earth do you think you need to get a dog and a Maine Coon cat? Those aren't required to have a baby."

MIAMI WAS TOO WARM. The airport was too crowded. Ugh. He dipped into a gift shop to get away from the masses of tourists. A large, stuffed toy caught his eye. It was an alligator with a Santa hat. His little boy needed that. Fifty dollars later, he carried the huge toy and his bag outside.

It was so damn bright and warm, and he didn't even need his coat. It was horrible. His phone rang, and he checked it. Andrew again. The man called him at least once a day. Harper didn't know how to make it stop. He'd tried talking to the omega and explaining that it was never going to happen, but he'd just ignored

Harper. Now, Harper just ignored him. It didn't seem to be working.

He rented a car, then plugged in Abuela's address. One of the newest Wilson family members was a man named Ray. He was one of Carter's best friends and was also pretty good at finding information. He hadn't even asked why Harper needed Ines Torres's address.

About thirty minutes later, Harper pulled into the drive of a worn apartment complex. According to Ray, Ines lived on the second floor, room 242B. Before he knew it, he stood in front of her door, hand raised to knock. He paused and thought about what he was going to do. What if she *did* stop loving Grey?

He knocked. If she wasn't the kind of person he thought she was, Grey would still have his family. He'd have Harper.

Ines opened the door. She was in her late sixties, but still young, just like his Grammy. Her salt and pepper hair was thick and rolled in a bun on top of her head. Her wrinkled brown face looked suspicious. "Who are you? I don't want to buy anything." A white, miniature poodle sat at her feet, judging him.

"My name is Harper," he said. "I'm a friend of—Whoa, okay."

She grabbed his arm and pulled him into a strong hug. "Mi corazón talks about you all the time," she said, stepping back and looking him up and down. "Come in and tell me what's wrong with my boy. I know there's something."

Harper sat on her old sofa and told her what he

knew. He tattled. Grey would be mad, but he needed someone. He needed Harper and Ines.

"Grey is pregnant? That horrible alpha abandoned him? My poor boy."

"You aren't mad at him, right?"

"Of course not! Why would you ask that?" She looked baffled.

Harper smiled. Grey wouldn't be losing anyone at all. "I think he was afraid of disappointing you."

"Estúpido!"

"I agree," Harper said. "Now, do you really want to move? Gramps, my grandpa, already found you a nice little house in Hobson Hills. It's in town and close to my cousin's bakery. My family owns it, so you won't be paying rent."

"I most certainly will pay rent," she said, looking around her cluttered home. "I'll start packing. I'm tired of this place and want to be near mi corazón."

"Would you like some help? I hired some movers for Grey, but I have a feeling he has less than I thought he would. They'll get to his place in another hour. I can send them on to you after."

She laughed. "He has books and his dolls. That's all. I could use any help you send. You're taking him home tonight?"

"Yes," he said. "We'll fly back home. I want him to get in to see the doctor."

Ines patted his cheek, smiling wide. "You're a good boy too. Just like my Grey. Now, go take care of him. I'll see you at the airport tonight."

CHAPTER 4

"That can't be right," Grey said. He held his phone to his ear and looked at the CSSDesign Awards website.

"Oh, it's right," Georgia Lenal said in his ear. "Lane entered the Hornston website three months ago. It won Website of the Month. I overheard Mr. Delwick bragging to a client. He thinks it'll win Website of the Year too."

"I designed that website," Grey said, shaking his head. "This can't be right."

"Grey, you're too naïve. Lane has been stealing your projects ever since you started. He calls you his assistant."

"This can't be right," he repeated.

"I have an appointment with Mr. Delwick today at 10:00 a.m., and I'm telling him."

"What if they fire me?"

"Why would they fire you? You're the one who's doing all the great work."

"Lane says that Delwick doesn't like omegas. He thinks they need constant guidance and can't be trusted. What if he thinks it's my fault?"

"Then he's a fucking idiot who deserves to lose you," Georgia said. "Listen, I've been his assistant for eleven years. I know the man, and he won't be mad at you. Hell, he has two omega sons that he adores. He is the least intolerant man I know."

"You promise? I really like this job, Georgia."

"I know you do, Grey, and you're really good at it. You have some serious talent, and Mr. Delwick won't want to lose that. It's time this company treated you right."

"Okay. I trust you," he said, voice small. What would he do if he lost his job? He had baby boy to think about now too.

"It'll be okay, Grey. I'll figure things out today and call you tomorrow at noon. Don't answer any calls from Lane. As soon as he figures out what's going on, he'll try to call you and bully you into submission. Just answer for my number, okay?"

"Thanks, Georgia."

He hung up, then grabbed his pillow, staring at the screen. This was a nightmare. His life was a nightmare. The only good things were baby boy, Harper, and Abuela. He sighed and got up. He needed another ice pack for his nose. The heating pad felt better, but it was too swollen. At least Dorian was at work now.

Walking into the living room, he heard knocking on the door. It was only 9:00 a.m. Could his day get any worse? He waddled to the door and pulled it open. His eyes widened, and he slammed the door shut. No. This wasn't real.

"Come on, Grey," Harper said through the door. "Let me inside."

"You aren't real," Grey yelled. "Go away."

"I have doughnuts," he said. "Plus, bacon and egg biscuits."

Grey's belly rumbled. Baby boy was hungry. This sucked. It really did. He whined and opened the door again. "You aren't supposed to be here," he said.

Harper looked gorgeous in real life. He was tall with broad shoulders. His dark brown hair was short and neat, begging for Grey to run his hands through it. Harper's eyes were a soft, sweet brown, instantly calming the anxiety swirling in his chest.

"Our video call didn't cut off last night. I'm sorry, but I eavesdropped and watched you all night."

Grey watched him in horror, thinking of everything that had happened. Dorian, his nose, his doughnut song, the phone call with Abuela. "You saw the doughnut song?"

"Yes," Harper nodded. "It was my favorite part."

"I also have a taco song," Grey said, then covered his face. "What is wrong with me?"

"You need to eat breakfast, then we'll go get your nose checked out," Harper said, leading him to a chair in the kitchen. "I'll get you a bag packed. The movers will be here in another twenty minutes, and they can pack up what's left."

"Movers? What's happening?" Grey started in on the first biscuit.

"You and Abuela are moving to Hobson Hills. I hired movers to pack up your room, but we're flying out tonight."

"Abuela? You talked to Abuela?"

"Yes. She loves you very much, but she's upset you didn't tell her. She doesn't hate you, and she's not disappointed in you, sunshine," Harper said. He walked to Grey's room, pushing the busted door open with a scowl. "I really hope Dorian shows up before we leave."

Grey followed behind him, munching on a second biscuit. Harper didn't hate him. Abuela didn't hate him. Baby boy was liking the biscuits. Should he move to Maine? He had to leave here anyway, and Harper didn't hate him. Harper *didn't* hate him. *Harper didn't hate him.*

His brain was broken.

Harper opened his closet, pulling a big duffel bag out. "Okay, so is there anything that you don't trust the movers with? They'll be careful, so your books and Pop! collection should be okay, but is there anything you'd rather just bring with us?"

Grey opened the bag of doughnuts, nodding. He pointed to his closet. "There's a box in the very back corner. It's blue." He munched on mini doughnuts.

Harper dug out the blue box. "What's in here?"

"Photo albums, my dad's journals, my mom's jewelry, and Rue's favorite t-shirt," he said and looked away. "Their ashes."

"We'll take good care of it," Harper said. "It can be my carry on. Anything else?"

Grey's mouth was full, cheeks puffed out. He pointed to the top of the closet. A big, ragged teddy bear sat on top of more boxes. He swallowed. "Cindy Bear."

"Cindy Bear comes with, got it," Harper said, reaching up and tugging her down. "Anything else?"

Grey shook his head, mouth full again. Those were his most prized possessions. Harper nodded. "Okay, so let's get you a couple of warm outfits to get you by until your things arrive." He looked through the closet. "Um, Grey, do you have warm clothes? Maybe a sweatshirt? A thick coat?"

"It's Florida, Harper," Grey said. "I have long-sleeved shirts, thin sweaters, and a light coat. None of those fit me right now."

"You can wear one of my sweaters, and we'll get you a coat. Do you have sweatpants? What are your warmest pants?"

Grey pulled out a pair of fuzzy pants with unicorns on them. They were thick and stretchy. Harper grinned, setting them aside. "What about boots," Harper asked.

"My preggo feet don't do boots," Grey said. "They don't do anything but flipflops."

"That's a problem, sunshine. There's at least two feet of snow on the ground right now."

"My feet won't fit in my shoes, Harper. It's not happening."

"We'll stop at the store while we're out." He started stuffing clothes in the bag. Grey finished the doughnuts and then opened his underwear drawer. He stuffed them all in the bag, blushing when a lacy pair of manties fell on the floor.

Harper bent and picked them up, holding the black cloth up. Somehow, the man managed to grin and blush at the same time. "I like these," he said.

"Oh, do you want a pair?" Grey raised a brow. He refused to be embarrassed for his love of pretty underthings.

"If you'll wear them, then yeah, I do," Harper said. "I'm too attached to boxer briefs to wear anything this constricting, but they sure are nice."

Grey snorted and cupped his belly. "Trust me, you don't want to see me in my underwear right now."

Harper pulled Grey's hands to his side, then ran his hands over his belly. "There's a baby in here, Grey. You're growing a human being. A little boy. You are absolutely beautiful, sunshine."

"Harper," Grey said, reality setting in. "You're really here, aren't you?"

"I am," he said.

"I'm moving to Maine?"

"Yes. We're flying out tonight."

Grey nibbled his lip, thinking hard. He knew Harper, knew about his family. They didn't know him though. Didn't know what a mess he was. "I'll go, but you have to promise me one thing."

"Anything," Harper said immediately.

"Don't tell your family yet," Grey said. "After all you've told me about them, I really want to be more put together before I meet them. I don't want them to think I'm an omega whore," he said, the last word feeling dirty and heavy on his tongue.

"I don't want to hear that word from you," Harper said, anger filling his eyes. "You aren't a whore."

"Okay," Grey said. He didn't think he was, people just kept telling him he was. "You'll promise? You'll wait to say anything to your family?"

"If that's what you need, but I know they want to meet you, and they already love you."

"Please," Grey said.

"Okay. Let's get you to the doctor, so he can look at that nose. We'll go ahead and load this in the rental."

Grey put on his flip flops, loaded up his laptop, and grabbed his work bag. Harper promptly took the two bags and added it to his load. Grey looked around his room. For a long time, it was his sanctuary. Now, though, it was just a room. Surprisingly, he wasn't scared. Harper came back in, smiled, and grabbed his blue box. Harper was here now.

Grey went to his bathroom and packed up the essentials, then met Harper at the door. Two men in moving uniforms stood just inside, talking to the alpha.

"What all do you need moved outside your room, sunshine?"

"Dorian won't like it if I take anything else," Grey said nervously.

"Fuck that asshole," one of the movers said, looking at his nose. "What do you want?"

Grey pointed to a chair in the corner of the living room. Dorian liked to pile his workout gear on it. "That chair, there. It was my great-grandmother's. That's all."

"Yes, sir," the other man said, nodding. "We'll have

things packed up within two hours and get over to the second address."

"Oh, what about my scooter?" Grey loved his bright red scooter. It was so cheerful and fun. Of course, he hadn't been able to ride it for the last few months, but still.

"We'll load it in one of the trucks. Is it the red one out front?"

"Yes," Grey said, nodding enthusiastically. They were doing this. He was moving to Maine.

Fuck a duck.

CHAPTER 5

*H*arper carried Grey's bags and rolled Ines's suitcase behind him. Grey hugged the stuffed alligator as he waddled toward their gate. Ines walked beside him.

"Mi corazón is having a baby. I can't believe you didn't tell me. I would have moved you in and pampered you. You won't cook for yourself, and I know you love my tamales."

"I'm sorry, Abuela."

"I forgive you, but don't let it happen again. I love you and always will, but you even missed Thanksgiving. This cannot happen again."

Harper grinned as he turned in the bigger pieces of luggage. He got the two seated at the gate and ran to the restroom, pulling out his phone and dialing.

"Hi, sweetie," Bennett said. "Have you all left yet?"

"We're at the airport now," he said. "I need you to do something. Tell everyone to act like they don't know

"

he's coming. He made me promise not to tell you about it yet."

"So, we shouldn't meet you at the airport then?"

"Probably not."

"Can I still fill up the fridge? I need to feed him, sweetie. I need to."

Harper laughed. "Yeah, Papa. Food would be appreciated. I'm hoping he'll settle quickly, then you all can get to loving him."

"I will restrain myself as long as possible. Hannah went ahead and picked up the cat and dog. Dr. Grover was happy to help. He may have sent a little something extra, but Hannah just couldn't say no."

"Of course, she couldn't," Harper said. "She's as bad as Carter."

"It's why we have four dogs, three cats, and five horses. Well, enjoy your something extra. Love you, sweetie."

"Love you too," he said, then hung up. He hated the thought of keeping his family away from Grey.

He picked up some bottled water and sat next to his omega, handing out the water. Grey leaned his head on Harper's shoulder, yawning. His sunshine was exhausted already. Harper knew he hardly ever left the house, so all this activity was draining him.

"Harper, tell me about this house you've found for me," Ines said.

"It's in town and has a little back yard for Sophia," he said nodding to Ines' dog. She currently sat in a little pet carry-on bag. "There are two bedrooms and one bathroom, so it's a little small, but my Aunt Anna thinks it's adorable. It has pretty blue siding and a big bay window. Oh, and a small fireplace in the living room. I made sure it was stocked before flying down."

"It sounds lovely," Ines said. "I've been wanting something new for a while now but was waiting until mi corazón settled down."

"Abuela," Grey said. "You should never wait on me to do anything." He looked a little rough with the splint on his bruised nose.

"We're family," she said. "Don't forget it."

Harper took Grey's hand, squeezing it. "Just accept it, sunshine."

The flight was short, with only one stop, and they drove into Hobson Hills just before midnight. Harper pulled into the garage of Ines's new house. He unloaded her bags as Grey and Ines looked around.

"Your car and two U-Hauls will be here in about three days. The movers said they planned on booking it, and, luckily, the weather is cooperating."

"It's snowing," Grey said. "Won't they get stuck?"

His new boots looked ridiculous with his fuzzy unicorn pants tucked into them. He wore a knit hat with ear flaps and fox ears. Grey had picked it out himself and adored it. Harper knew his cousin Ernie would enjoy knitting all kinds of goofy hats and scarves for Grey.

"It's snow, not quicksand," Harper said. "You Floridians are so cute."

"Grey, don't stick your tongue out at him. It's rude, mi corazón," Ines said. "Harper, I love this house. Do you think the owner would sell it to me if Grey does decide to settle here for good?"

"I can guarantee he would," Harper said, thinking of Gramps and his need to keep his family close. "Now, the backyard is completely fenced in, so Sophia can run and romp to her heart's content. I also made sure the fridge was stocked. Do you need anything else before Grey and I head out?"

"No, sweet boy," she said, patting his cheek. "I saw the lovely quilt on the bed and the plants in the kitchen. You did very well."

"We'll come by and pick you up tomorrow," Harper said, hugging her. "We'll take you to the grocery store, and I'll show the two of you around town."

"Wonderful," she said. "Now get out of here. My boy needs sleep."

Harper looked at Grey. He was stretched out on his side on the couch, eyes sleepy. Yep. Time to get his omega home. "Come on, sunshine," Harper said. "Let's get home. I have a couple surprises for you and a very comfy bed."

"Okay, but you have to help me up," he said.

Harper chuckled, then pulled him up, ushering him to the door. After helping him back in the Jeep, Harper set out for home.

"There's Farm Fresh," he said as they passed the store. "Right here is where my parents, brother, and sister live. If you ever need anything, and I'm not around, Papa is almost always home. Plus, they keep a spare key under a loose rock on the left side of the stairs in the back, okay?"

"Why would I need to get into their house without them being there?"

"I don't know. If I get eaten by a bear and you need someone to make you dinner?"

"Oh my god! Are there a lot of bears here? Could you really get eaten? We can live in Florida, just don't swim in the lakes."

Harper laughed, pleased that Grey was thinking *we*. "It's just like anywhere. You need to be alert of your surroundings. It's a beautiful place," he said. "In the winter, everything looks bare, but it's a quiet and peaceful haven. Spring comes, and things get chaotic, both in nature and at the store. All the cousins try to pitch in and help Elijah collect and make maple syrup for the store. Somehow, he still ends up doing most of it. This year, though, this year will be my year."

Grey giggled. "How dare he do all that work! What a horrible person."

"I know, right? Then we plant the gardens in late spring. Summer is all about harvesting and canning. I try to work in the fields at least twice a week. Then fall has more harvesting."

"You still manage to build your stuff while doing all of that?"

"Of course. All the Wilsons pitch in with the farm and store. It spreads the work out, so while it sounds like a lot, it's not too bad."

"I'll be happy to help too," Grey said. "Once I've settled in. At least, I can if your family won't mind teaching me how to do all that stuff."

"We'd love the help," he said, pulling into his

driveway. "Here's home. Shawn was watching things for me but headed home earlier, since we landed on time. I asked Hannah to find me a couple of things, so I know I have two presents for you inside, but I don't know what they'll be for sure."

"You told Hannah I was coming?" His voice rose higher and higher with each word.

"Not exactly. I just asked her to find two specific things." For Grey. Oh fuck.

"Okay," he said. "I'm sorry to be a pain, and I really am looking forward to meeting your family. I just need a little time to adjust."

"I completely understand," Harper said. Fuck, he felt like shit for lying to Grey. He couldn't do it. Fuck. "Okay, Grey, I need to be honest here. Please don't be mad."

Grey's face paled and his eyes grew big. "You're married, aren't you? Oh god, I can't believe this is happening."

Harper blinked. "No. I'm not married. Why would you think that? No. I just… Before you asked me not to, I'd already told my parents and grandparents that you were coming. I've talked to them, and they've agreed to keep their distance for a bit, but they know you're here. Hannah knew she was picking out two presents for you. I'm so sorry. Please don't hate me."

"Oh, thank god you're not married," Grey said, sighing. He rolled his eyes. "I'm not exactly happy you already told them, but I know how close you all are. I should have realized you already had."

"My dad told me to kidnap you months ago. Papa talked me into restraining myself."

Grey giggled. "You are such a doof. Come on, I have to pee."

"Wait. I'll help you out," Harper said. He jumped out and ran around the Jeep. He opened the door and picked his omega up, slamming the door with his hip.

"Harper," Grey squealed, wrapping his arms around his neck. "I weigh like a thousand pounds."

"You are just perfect, sunshine," Harper said, carrying him up the porch steps.

"You really are a doof. I can't wait to see your house in the daylight. It looks like a bunch of shadows right now."

Harper set him on his feet in front of the door. "I'll give you the official tour tomorrow," he said and opened the door.

Grey walked in, then came to a full stop, shrieking. "Oh my god, they're so adorable."

He ran through the door, heading straight for the three animals spread out in Harper's living room.

A large, gray Maine Coon sat in Harper's recliner, fuzzy face solemn as he watched the white and black miniature piglet and the fluffy white Samoyed-Husky mix puppy sleep on a dog bed near the fireplace. The two babies curled up together. So, that was the extra something Dr. Grover sent. Hmm.

Grey picked up the cat, cuddling the huge beast to him as he stared down at the sleeping babies. "Are they mine, Harper? You said you only had the horses and your chickens. Did you have Hannah find them for me?"

Looking into his sweet, golden-brown eyes, Harper made a note to buy Hannah another Christmas present. The girl did good. "I did. Do you like them? I know they'll be a lot to deal with when the baby comes, but, remember, I'm here too. We can do this together, okay?"

"Together? You're the best friend in the whole world," Grey said. "You have no idea how alone I was. I would have handled it, because I had too, but I was so scared. Thank you, Harper."

Friends. Grey said he was his friend. Harper smiled weakly and nodded. "I'll always be here for you, Grey. Come on. I'll show you your room and you can get to bed. These two look comfortable right where they are."

Grey followed behind him, carrying the cat. He slowly climbed the stairs and made it to his room. "Harper, this is beautiful," he said, spinning around the corner bedroom.

The room was warm and cozy. All the furniture in the whole house was made by him or Gramps, and he took a lot of pride in his home. Soon, it would be Grey's home too, and they wouldn't just be friends. He'd be patient though. He could wait.

CHAPTER 6

Grey woke up the next morning, feeling rested and full of energy. The house was so warm, and he could see the snow falling outside his window. Tiny, the Maine Coon, curled up against his back, easing the normal morning ache. He hadn't felt this safe and at peace in years. Ideas for a new children's book spurred his imagination, but he needed to explore his new home.

He clumsily climbed out of bed, dislodging Tiny, and stretched. Spotting his bag on the window seat, he quickly put his few belongings away. The rest of his stuff would arrive in a few days, but he had the important things. After a quick snuggle, he set Cindy Bear against the pillows on the window seat.

The blue crate was pushed to the back of the closet. He hadn't opened it since the day a kind neighbor helped him pack it. He knew every item in there, and one day soon, he'd have to deal with it. The three small urns would need to come out, but not today. After a quick shower, he dressed in a clean pair of jogging pants and a t-shirt. Stopping by Harper's room, he stole a huge, warm sweater and a pair of thick socks, then headed downstairs, Tiny beside him.

Harper's home was gorgeous, if a little bare. The first level was log walls and high ceilings with rough beams. The wood floors somehow managed to contrast well with the walls, and Harper had a huge, off-white shag rug in front of the fireplace. Each piece of furniture was a gorgeous and comfortable work of art. He recognized Harper's touch on a lot of the pieces, but some were made by someone else. Intriguing.

Grey ran his fingers along the kitchen table, admiring the large open space. The counter tops were marble and the cabinets were oak. He opened the pantry door and found three labeled plastic tubs right next to the entrance. He opened the one labeled cat and got a scoop for Tiny. When the big cat started eating, Grey heard little clicks on the hardwood floors, heading for the kitchen.

Quick little squeals and barks proceeded Butterball the piglet and Opal the puppy. The two came to a stop and stared at Grey, curiosity clear in their bright eyes.

"Are you babies hungry? I have some food for you little bits." Grey fed them, singing to them as he did. His own belly rumbled loudly. "Time for me to eat too." He opened the fridge, gasping in happiness. "Dear lord of yummy food, thank you for your gifts," he said in awe.

Someone, Grey suspected Harper's papa, had filled the fridge with clearly labeled containers of delicious looking food. There were soups and a casserole, towering sandwiches and homemade egg salad. So much yumminess. He opened the freezer and squealed, sounding remarkably like Butterball. The freezer was full of pre-cooked, homemade meals. Harper's family was entirely too amazing.

He grabbed the egg salad and one of the sandwiches, setting them on the counter. Then he went back in for some veggies and diced fruit. Plate made and food returned to the fridge, Grey sat at the table and dug in. Humming happily, he watched the snow fall outside the picture window. He yelped and jumped when a face appeared in the bottom, knitted cap perched on the girl's head.

Her eyes darted around the room, freezing when she saw Grey. He waved, and the girl disappeared. The backdoor opened, and someone stomped their feet in the mudroom before coming in the kitchen.

"Hi, Grey," the girl said. "I know we're supposed to leave you alone, but I just couldn't. I had to know if you liked the animals Doc and I picked out."

"Hannah, right?"

She grinned, revealing the gap in her front teeth. Definitely a Wilson. Her long brown hair was loosely braided in pigtails, and her bright green eyes sparkled. "That's me!"

"I love Tiny, Butterball, and Opal. Thank you for picking them out for me."

"I'm glad," she said, sighing in relief. She grabbed one of his carrots, munching thoughtfully. "So, you're going to be here for good, right?"

"Uh, I don't know for sure," Grey said. "I'm kind of a mess and still trying to figure everything out." He got up and dug around in the fridge again, putting together another plate. He set it in front of Hannah, and she smiled, then took a big bite of the sandwich.

"Do you like it here?"

"Of course," he said. "Harper's home is beautiful, and, most importantly, Harper is here. You know how wonderful he is. He's my best friend."

"Friend, huh? He's okay, I guess," she said, shrugging. "He may be wonderful, but he can be stubborn, overprotective, and annoying."

Grey laughed and waved her words away. "That's all brothers, Hany."

"Hany? I like it," she said, smirking. "Anyway, you'll figure it out. After we finish eating, do you want me to introduce you to Dumpling and Boon?"

"That would be great. I don't know where Harper is, but he's told me so much about those two."

"He's probably in his shop." She polished off the cut-up veggies and pushed her plate back. "Come on, let's get the babies."

She ran to the closet next to the front door and rummaged around. Grey peeked in behind her. There was a ridiculously large number of knitted items, ranging from hats and scarfs to little sweaters perfect for a baby piglet or puppy.

"Where did these all come from? They look homemade." His tone may have been slightly jealous. He didn't like the idea of some omega sewing things for his Harper. Shit, he meant Harper, just Harper.

Hannah eyed him, pulling out a couple of small sweaters. "This stuff? An omega from town made them for Harper. He really likes him."

"Oh, really? I guess he doesn't like the idea of another omega staying with Harper, huh?" Well, he could suck it. Grey was never leaving Harper. Never!

"Well, you guys are just friends, right? I don't think he'd mind," Hannah said innocently. Together, the two of them wrestled the sweaters onto Butterball and Opal. She pushed a large coat at him too. "Wear this, okay? Your jacket's like toilet paper. Why would you wear toilet paper in the snow?"

Grey rolled his eyes and pulled the giant coat on. "This coat is huge, but I love it. It's mine now."

"Well, to be honest," Hannah said. "You're a little huge. Plus, that's one of Gramps's old coats. They make the rounds. I know he'd be all gruff and happy that you're wearing it." She helped him into his boots.

"I hope so, since it's mine now." He hugged Butterball close and pulled the little beanie down around her ears. One was black, and the other was white. The cuteness was too much.

Hannah carried Opal and Tiny followed behind them. "You waddle," she said. "You actually waddle."

"Why, Hany? Why would you say that?"

She held his arm, helping him down the icy steps. "I can't help it. You're so damn adorable."

"I don't think you're supposed to say damn."

"I'm thirteen, Grey, and you're not Papa."

They walked to a large, red barn near the fenced-in pasture behind the house. Tiny hopped through the snow, burrowing and rolling. Hannah pulled open the door, and they slipped in, and Grey heard a loud buzzing noise. They walked into a large room packed full of wood piles and half-finished projects.

Harper stood at a large machine, shaping wood. The buzzing stopped as he finished the piece. He looked up, seeing them, and turned the machine off. He pushed up his glasses, smiling widely.

"Hey guys," he said. "Did you sleep okay, Grey? I checked on you before getting to work, and you were out."

"I did," Grey said, looking at Harper's project. "What are you making?"

"The baby needs a cradle," Harper said, shrugging. "I'll get it put together today, then finish it up tomorrow. Then I'll get started on the rest."

Grey looked at the smooth wood. Harper was making his baby boy a cradle. He sniffed, trying to keep the tears at bay. "The rest?"

"We'll need a rocker for you and some bookshelves, a dresser, and a toy box for the baby's room. Gramps and Dad are coming over tomorrow while you're at Ines's house, and we're going to paint the nursery. Speaking of, I'll need you to pick out a color. I was thinking, maybe yellow and cream. What do you think?"

The tears came, and he couldn't hold back the sobs. "You broke him, Harper," Hannah said, setting Opal down and hugging Grey.

Harper looked terrified. "What did I say? What's

wrong? Whatever's wrong, I'll fix it, sunshine. I promise."

"Nothing's wrong," Grey said through his tears. "It's just… You're taking care of the baby, making him something special."

"Thank god," Hannah said. "Happy tears."

Grey nodded. They were extremely, unbelievably happy tears.

Harper cupped his face, eyes searching his own. "Anything I can do for you and the baby, I will, sunshine." He kissed his forehead and released him. "Now, think of a good color. We'll pick it up while we're in town today. I thought we'd leave in a couple hours and go check on Ines."

"I'll come too," Hannah said. "You need to get some clothes. Now come on. Dumpling and Boon are waiting."

"Get the eggs while you're there, Hannah, okay?" Harper put his safety glasses back on and picked up a new piece of wood.

"Yeah, okay," she said, picking up Opal and leading the way into the barn.

Dumpling and Boon stuck their noses over their gates. "Look at those little noses," Grey said, rushing forward. He petted their noses. "They're so soft."

Hannah topped off their hay. "Doc has a bunch of Angora bunnies, you know. We could build some pens near the chickens, and you could harvest their fur for Ernie to make yarn with. We could use their manure for the gardens. Their original owner passed away, so Doc is hunting for homes for them."

"Would Harper mind?"

"If you wanted it, he'd want it."

"I don't know, Hany," he said, nibbling his lip. "On one hand, I have three new pets and a baby on the way. On the other hand, I've always liked rabbits. When I was a kid, our neighbor had a shed full of rabbits. She'd show them at fairs and breed them to sell."

"I'll talk to Doc," Hannah said. "Maybe if no one else steps up, you guys could take them on, and I could help out. I'll be over all the time when the baby gets here anyway."

Grey watched Dumpling sniff Butterball. "Why would you be over all the time? Not that I'd mind. I like you."

"Because it's a baby," she said, rolling her eyes. "Papa will be all over that baby, and he's the one who cooks. I go where the food goes." Grey couldn't stop laughing, so Hannah left him and went for the eggs.

A couple of hours later, the three of them, along with Butterball and Opal, piled into Harper's Jeep. Tiny seemed completely unconcerned with being left behind. He was sprawled out on the kitchen floor, napping in the sunlight.

"Everything's so pretty," Grey said, nose pressed to the window. "These trees are huge, and good god, look at all the snow. I won't be able to ride my scooter for a while, huh?"

"Nope," Harper said. "We have the Jeep though. Might need to think about getting another vehicle too."

"There's Farm Fresh, Grey," Hannah said. "Aunt Anna runs the place."

The store was decorated for Christmas, and a ton of cars were parked outside. Looked like things were busy. Right behind the store was a large Christmas tree farm. Even though it was ten in the morning on a weekday, there were people walking through it.

Wait, it was ten in the morning on a weekday.

"Hannah, why aren't you in school?" Grey looked behind him in time to catch her guilty expression.

"Uh, we didn't meet today?"

"Hany," he said. "Are you skipping?"

"Don't tell Dad and Papa," she said, sighing. "I just really wanted to meet you."

"Oh, you are in big trouble," Harper said, amused.

"Harper," she said, begging. "Please."

"I'm dropping you off, and I won't say anything to the dads, but you had best think of a good excuse or you know the school will call them."

"Okay," she said. "Just make sure Grey gets some new clothes. He looks stupid."

"I'm right here, Hany. Right here."

"Love you," she said, smiling sweetly.

"I feel it," Grey said wryly.

Harper watched the screen as the doctor spoke. He could see the baby. Oh god, he could see the baby. He was right there in Grey's belly. Ines grabbed his hand, squeezing it.

"Breathe, Harper," she said, amused.

"Well, your little boy looks just fine. I looked over the chart your doctor faxed, and the only thing you need to work on is eating better. You need to be eating more and eating healthier foods."

"He'd eat doughnuts for every meal if he could," Ines said, rubbing Grey's shoulders.

"What's the due date," Grey asked, looking guilty at the mention of doughnuts.

"He'll be knocking at the door within three weeks."

"Right before Christmas," Harper said in wonder. His boy might be a Christmas baby.

"Yep," Doctor Richards said, grinning. "Now, like I said, just eat a lot and eat well. If anything seems off, come in immediately."

"Okay," Grey said, sitting up. "Thank you." He turned big eyes toward Harper. "Can we get some lunch? All that clothes shopping made me hungry."

Harper laughed. "Turn those eyes off. Of course, we can get lunch. We'll go to Cozy Kitchen."

"I'll leave you two to it," Ines said. "I'm meeting Laurel at the yarn store. I'm joining the knitting club."

Harper frowned. The name Laurel sounded familiar. Oh, yeah. Grammy's name was Laurel. "Did Grammy and Gramps already get ahold of you?"

"Laurel es un ángel," Ines said, smiling.

"Abuela, will you get me some stuff to start knitting? I need to make some scarves, and it can't be that hard. Any omega could do it," Grey said, glaring at Harper. He couldn't think of anything he'd done to make Grey mad.

"Of course, mi corazón," Ines said, chuckling. "Anything you need." Ines walked down the street toward the yarn store, and Harper and Grey continued toward the diner.

"Why do you want to take up knitting?"

"No reason," Grey said, nose in the air. "Anyway, Georgia texted me earlier."

"What did she say?"

"She said she'd call tonight. That's it," Grey said, looking worried.

"Well, if Delwick doesn't take care of it, you can find a job somewhere else. Your talent belongs to you, not them. Hey, you could always keep working on your children books," Harper said. "No matter what, I'm here, Grey."

"Thanks, Harper," he said, linking arms with Harper and leaning his head on the alpha's shoulder as they walked.

When they reached the diner, Harper's cousin Abel had his face pressed to the window, watching them. He frantically shook his head, mouthing something. Weirdo. They walked in and Harper looked for an empty spot, growling when he saw a familiar face seated at the bar.

Andrew.

Abel popped in front of them. "Hey, Grey," he said. "My name's Abel, and I'm one of Harper's many cousins. How about a booth in the back, near the window? Follow me." He grabbed Grey's arm and started tugging him toward the back.

"Harper," Andrew said, spinning around on his stool. "How's my hunky cocktease doing?"

"Damn it." Abel growled and tried to pull Grey to their table. Harper just ignored Andrew like he usually did.

"Excuse me?" Grey turned around, moving to block Harper from Andrew's sight.

Andrew looked him up and down, looking disgusted. "I finally understand, Harper. You like them fat. That explains everything."

Harper snarled, trying to get around his omega. Abel stood beside Grey, blocking him in.

"Wait," Grey said, pushing back and leaning into Harper. He wrapped his arms around his omega, wondering what he was up to. "You're Andrew, right? The college boyfriend?"

Andrew smirked. "I'm hard to forget."

"Yeah, I mean you were such an ignorant asshole," Grey said. "Luckily, most people aren't like that."

"What did you say?" Andrew stood, looking around. The regulars of the diner tried to hide their smiles, but their amusement was clear enough. "I'm not the one who couldn't get it up. We dated for two months and what did I get? Nothing."

"Nothing? You got two months of Harper's time," Grey said. "It's not his fault you weren't right for him. Jesus, man, move on."

Andrew pushed into Grey's face. "I'll move on after I get that cock in my ass."

"Do you know what sexual harassment is?" Abel watched the other omega in disbelief. "Harper, you didn't tell us this guy was a complete whacko."

"Seriously," Grey agreed. "Harper's more than a dick."

"Sir," Mrs. Bethel said, voice prim and proper, perfectly matching her old schoolmarm look. "I'm going to have to ask you to leave. You're disturbing our guests." She grabbed Andrew's arm in a tight grip and dragged him to the door. "Your bill is covered. Just go."

Andrew stalked off, glaring at Grey and Harper. Unfortunately, that wasn't the first encounter Harper had suffered through with him. Justin was even worse in some ways. He had been Harper's boyfriend all through high school, and his words hurt more than Andrew's.

Mrs. Bethel came back in, tsking. "The Wilsons are a dramatic bunch, that's for sure."

"Hey," Harper said. "His behavior's not my fault."

"Oh, it never is the Wilsons' fault," she said, rolling her eyes. "Drama just follows you all."

"Ignore her," Abel said, pulling Grey to their table. "She's just grumpy today." He slid in beside Grey. "I'm taking my break," he yelled.

"I'm sorry, Grey," Harper said. "I know they're not supposed to bother you yet."

Abel looked affronted. "I'm never a bother."

Grey giggled. "It's fine. One at a time is turning out pretty well."

"Good," Abel said. "So tonight, do you want to come out with me? Not you, Harper, just Grey. Omegas only."

"Sure," Grey said, making Harper frown. "That sounds fun. It's been months since I went anywhere for fun."

Damn it. Now Harper couldn't sulk. "Where you two going?"

"Thought we'd go to the pub," Abel said as the waitress came over. After ordering, Abel continued. "Hobson Hills only has one bar, so it gets some traffic. Unfortunately, it's a crappy bar. The food sucks and the beer's disgusting, but it's somewhere to go."

"That sounds so fun," Grey said dryly. "I'm still in though."

After lunch, they walked down Main Street, arms linked again. Each house and business was decorated for Christmas, and Harper recognized more than a few of his wreathes. "How do you like Hobson Hills?"

"This town is beautiful," Grey said. "Most importantly, though, you're here."

Harper grinned. "Thanks," he said, then sighed. "I'm sorry about Andrew. Every time he sees me, he makes a scene. It's really embarrassing."

"He's an idiot," Grey said. "Don't worry about it." He looked at Harper curiously. "You know it's not your fault, right? Being demisexual is just part of who you are. If he doesn't get it after you told him, and he dated you for two months, that's on him."

"He kept saying that we had spent enough time together, so I should want him. I couldn't help what I didn't feel. Then he started listing off statistics about what was an appropriate amount of time to wait before having sex. The pressure just got harder and harder to deal with."

"That's not something you should have to deal with. No one should ever pressure their partner to act a certain way about sex."

"That's what Papa says," Harper said. "It was a couple of years ago, but Andrew still won't let it go. I know it's not normal."

"No," Grey agreed. "Something is definitely wrong with that man."

"So, you might run into Justin too," Harper said. "He's not as bad."

Grey laughed. "Of course. Well, you have me here now. I'll protect you."

"You need an omega to protect you?" Justin's bitter voice came from behind them, and Harper groaned.

"You must be Justin," Grey said, amused.

"How did you possibly knock up an omega when your dick hardly works?"

"Watch your mouth," Grey said angrily, amusement disappearing at the other omega's harsh words.

"Justin, just back off. Nothing about me is your business," Harper said, trying to diffuse the situation.

"Thank god it isn't. I have a real man now, not a joke like you."

"You would be the luckiest man in the world to have Harper, but you sure don't," Grey said. "So, go on to your *real man* and leave mine alone."

Harper couldn't help but grin. He knew Grey was just being protective, but he liked the way *mine* sounded on his tongue.

Justin rolled his eyes and sneered. "Like I care about him. I wasted high school on that limp-dicked asshole." He turned around and briskly walked away.

"Why are they so bitter? I mean, I know sex is important in a relationship, but it's not the only thing."

Harper looked down. "I've been described as cold and distant more times than I can count. It just takes me time to warm up to people, especially romantically."

"You're not cold or distant," Grey said.

"Not to you, but that took time too, remember?"

"Oh yeah. I thought you were super shy."

"You kept at me, though, making me laugh and pulling words out of me. I've never told someone that wasn't a family member that much about myself. Then one day, I just needed you, like air. Your face became necessary to my life."

Grey leaned up and kissed his cheek. Harper's heart

began beating faster. He had never felt like this before. With Justin, he had cared. After a year of dating, they'd had sex, but it was never enough, never as often as Justin wanted. With Andrew, it just hadn't happened. Grey was different, was special.

"You are so worth the time, Harper. Never doubt that."

"Thanks, sunshine. Let's go pick up Butterball and Opal. Ines gave you a spare key, right?"

"Yes," Grey said. "Do you think Sophia taught them anything while we were gone?"

"I hope she potty-trained Opal. How is it possible for Butterball to already be trained?"

"Pigs are smart. Opal… Well, Opal's really cute."

CHAPTER 8

"Are you and Harper a couple?" Abel's blond curls bounced as he danced to the music on the radio. Fifteen minutes ago, he'd pulled up in a purple Chevy Silverado. Harper had promptly pointed them to the Jeep, since it was easier for Grey to get in and out of.

"We're just friends," he said. Grey had just spent six hours trying to knit a fucking scarf for his friend. It was a lot harder than it looked.

"Sure," Abel said. "Friends."

Grey's phone rang, and he recognized Georgia's number. "I need to take this, okay? It's work."

"No problem." Abel turned down the radio.

"Georgia?"

"Hey, sweetie. I'm sorry I put you off earlier. I wanted to let the dust settle a bit, so I could give you the details."

"It's okay. What did Mr. Delwick say?"

"He was pissed and investigated immediately. I gave

him the drafts you sent me, showing it was your work. I showed him the log in information and timings. One of them showed that Lane was supposedly working on the website when he was in a meeting with Mr. Delwick."

"So, he didn't believe Lane?"

"Not for a moment. He's had problems with Lane for a while apparently. Now, Mr. Delwick contacted the CSSDesign Awards website and told them the wrong name was listed as the creator for the website. They fixed it, easy peasy."

"Oh my god," Grey said. "People know it's my website and that it won best website of the month?"

"Yes," she said, laughing. "Mr. Delwick wants to talk with you, and he'll call your cell tomorrow morning at nine. Will that be okay?"

"Of course. Georgia, I don't know how to thank you."

"Just keep doing what you're doing. You're a great designer and a sweet person."

"Lane called twenty-two times since noon yesterday. He's sent some really nasty texts and e-mails too."

"I want you to forward them to me, alright? Don't engage with the asshole. He's mad, and from what I overheard, he's trying to blame everything on you. He even tried to get Mr. Delwick to fire you for being an unwed, pregnant omega. Is this the fifties or something?"

"There are still a lot of people who would agree with him."

"Well, they're idiots, and Mr. Delwick is not one of them. I have to go, but remember, nine tomorrow."

"Okay, bye."

"Good news?" Abel asked.

"Yes," he said, smiling widely, almost giddy with relief. "My former supervisor stole credit for my work, and our boss just found out. He believed me, and I still have a job."

"Really good news," Abel said. "How did your supervisor take it?"

"He's really mad."

Abel pulled into the parking lot, and they saw The Irish Rose. It was a dump. The building was tiny and dilapidated. The sign hung at an angle, neon lights flashing on and off.

"Impressive, right?" Abel waggled his brows suggestively. "Wait until you see the inside."

The inside was even worse.

"I'm a little afraid to sit down," Grey said.

"A little dirt and grime won't hurt," Abel said, looking around for a seat. "Holy shit! That's Caden. He's Carter's older brother. I didn't know he was in town."

Grey followed Abel to a table in the corner. They sat at the alpha's table, and the man looked up, blinking slowly. "Huh?"

"Fuck me," Abel said in awe. "You're drunk, aren't you?"

"No," Caden said, shaking his head slowly. "Not drunk. No." The man was in his mid-thirties, with dark hair and eyes. Eyes that were a bit bloodshot and confused.

"You are so drunk," Abel said.

"Are you okay?" Grey grabbed the man's beer and set it away from him.

"No," Caden said, eyes tearing up.

"Oh, Caden," Abel said, grabbing his hand. "What's wrong?"

"I hate Carter," he mumbled. "He's free."

"Harper said Carter and his brothers were getting along really well now," Grey said. "Caden, what do you mean that he's free. He's married, so his freedom's all gone."

"As it should be," Abel said, nodding firmly.

"He gets to plumb stuff."

"I'm not sure what to say to that," Grey said.

"You mean he's a plumber?" Abel turned to Grey. "Carter kind of rebelled against his parents and joined the army. When he got out, he rebelled again and became a plumber."

"Being a plumber is freedom?"

"He chose it," Caden said, sniffing. "I can't go back. I won't. I'd rather die."

"Whoa there, buddy," Grey said, grabbing Caden's other hand. "Abel, go get us some coffee and water. We need to get him sobered up."

"On it." The blond ran to the bar.

"Don't make me go back. Please."

"Go back where?"

"To work. I don't want to law anymore."

"Oh yeah," Grey said. "Harper told me you all were lawyers. You don't like it?"

"Hate it."

"What does he hate," Abel said, pushing a cup of coffee toward the drunk man, then taking his hand again.

"Being a lawyer," Grey answered.

"Oh, my god," Abel said. "You didn't want to be a lawyer? Did your parents pressure you into it like they tried with Carter?"

Caden nodded. "I gave. He didn't, and now, he's happy."

"And you're not," Grey finished. "Oh, Caden."

"I'm a screwup," Caden said. "I'm garbage."

"Hey," Abel said. "You're not garbage, and you aren't the only screwup here."

"Abel! I know I'm a hot mess right now, but you don't have to point it out," Grey said.

The tiny blond laughed. "I wasn't talking about you, hot mess, but do tell."

"Oh," Grey said blushing. The other two men stared at him, waiting. "Well, if you hadn't noticed, I'm pregnant. The father dumped me and ran, then I met Harper and fell in love. We're just friends though. He deserves someone better than me."

"Grey," Abel said. "You're a great guy."

"No, I'm not," he said, tears filling his eyes. "I'm twenty-three years old, and I'm incapable of taking care of myself or the baby. I was renting a room, guys, for years. I'm eight months pregnant and had nothing prepared for the baby. All I did was avoid thinking about all the changes that were happening. I never face problems. I just pack them in a blue box and push them to the back of the closet."

"That's pacific," Caden said, squinting at him.

"He means specific," Abel said, watching Grey closely. "What blue box are you avoiding?"

"My parents and little brother died when I was seventeen," Grey said, surprising himself. "I packed them up in a box. Their ashes, their belongings, their memories. Harper is the only one I've even talked about them to. Every time we talked, he would always ask about my childhood."

"Time to stretch it," Caden said, trying to get his beer.

"Huh?" Abel grabbed the beer and downed it. "Bad, Caden. No beer for you."

"It's time for Grey to grow. To stretch," Caden said, pouting.

"That's a good point," Abel said. "Dad always says you have to love yourself to be able to love someone else. Maybe you need to get your shit together. Think about the baby and the future." He pulled Grey into a hug. "Time to deal with the past. Then, you'll realize how utterly wonderful you are."

Grey smiled, eyes wet. "Yeah, okay. What about Caden? What are we going to do? If you don't want to be a lawyer, then it's time to make a change."

"Yeah, Caden," Abel said. "What do you want to be when you grow up?"

"It's embarrassing," the alpha said, blushing.

Grey thought he might be sobering up. "Tell us. Tell us now."

He and Abel leaned forward, staring Caden into submission.

"I write romance novels," he said. "I'm published and everything."

"Oh. My. God," Abel said. "Caden Benson, severe and stern lawyer, is a secret romance novelist? My life is complete."

"What's your pen name? I love romance novels," Grey said. "My mom adored Victorian romances. She named me and my brother after characters in her favorite. Greyson and Rupert. Blah!"

Caden's mouth tried to smile, but Grey thought maybe it didn't know how. "That's actually great." His shoulders slumped. "I'm Roxanne Baxter."

Abel and Grey squealed in unison, bouncing in their seats. "I love your books," Grey said. "I just read the newest release!"

"Me too, me too," Abel said, hugging Caden. "Thank you for being so awesome, Caden."

The alpha blushed a deep red, and his mouth tried to smile again. "I really like doing it, and I've made alright money."

"Then why are you still lawyering?" Abel shook his head. "If you don't like something, why still do it?"

"It's not a bad profession, and our firm has done a lot of good."

"But?" Grey moved his chair close to Caden's other side and nudged him.

"I hate it," Caden said. "I hate it so much. When I

walk into the office, I feel like I'm suffocating. I can't go back. I just can't."

"Then don't," Grey said. "Hire or promote someone in your place and write romance novels. Write them faster, okay? I need them."

"You make it sound so easy," he said, sighing.

"Isn't that the problem," Abel asked sadly. "You can know what will make you happy and whole, but doing it, taking that step, is hard."

"What about you, Abel?" Grey asked. "You were about to tell us how you're a screwup. What gives? You're a Wilson. I don't think your genetics will let you be a screwup."

"That's it exactly," Abel said, slumping in his seat. "I'm a Wilson. We know what we want out of life. We go after it and make it happen. By the age of sixteen, every single Wilson knew what they wanted to do with their life. College, crafting, whatever."

"Okay?"

"I'm a waiter," he said. "I don't know what I want to do with my life. I kind of just want to brew beer."

"Well, you're young," Caden said. "You have time."

"I'm twenty. Hannah is thirteen and already knows she wants to be a veterinarian."

"Hannah is just Hannah," Grey said. "That's one Wilson."

"Elijah knew he wanted to learn about investing at ten and graduated with a masters at eighteen. Zoe wanted a bakery when she was five. Janelle always wanted to be a librarian. Evan knew he wanted to be a doctor when he was fourteen, and Ernie knew he wanted to teach elementary school when he was six. Six! Milly is just sixteen, but she knows she wants to take over managing Farm Fresh when Aunt Anna retires. Allison is fourteen. Yesterday she told me she's decided to run the gardens for the farm when she finishes college. She's going to major in agriculture. Finally, Shawn's already apprenticing with the local mechanic, and Noah decided to open an Equine Therapy center for veterans. That's all the fucking Wilsons. All of them."

"You're all over-achievers too," Caden said. "Everyone pitches in with the store and the farm."

"At least I help with that," Abel said. "I'm still a wreck though." He leaned forward, whispering. "I still live at home, and I'm lying to my parents about school. They think I'm finishing up my business degree, but I majored in brewing."

"Abel, I may have just heard about them from Harper, but I know they'd want you to be happy. You don't have to lie."

"I know," he said. "Look at me though. I have no job prospects, don't know what I want to do anyway, and like to brew beer. I'm the most pathetic Wilson in the world."

"Brewing beer, huh?" Caden rested his head on Abel's shoulder. "You're young and have time, but if you want to make some decisions, then we'll do it."

Grey smiled at the two men, his two friends. "We'll do it together. We'll help each other."

After a few hours of disgusting drinks and stale pretzels, the three men walked to their cars, the two omegas each holding one of Caden's arms. "Tonight was a good night," Caden said.

"Stupid fucking dog."

An angry voice came from behind the dumpster. Grey heard a thump, then a dog's whimper. He growled, letting go of Caden and rushing to the dumpster, his two friends easily keeping pace with him. A grungy beta was about to kick a huge, cowering dog.

"Stop it," Grey said, flashing back to every pinch, push, kick, and punch that Dorian had given him. He'd taken it, hadn't fought back. He was done with that shit now. The man turned and glared at them.

"Fuck you, fat ass," he said. "This is my dog, and I'll do what I want. The useless piece of shit won't do what I say."

Grey and Abel both took a step forward, but Caden grabbed their arms. "I completely understand," the alpha said. Abel and Grey both stared at him in disbelief. "Pets can be a pain in the ass."

"This one sure is," the man said, scowling at the dog. "He's a big, fucking baby. I should have gotten the Rottweiler like I wanted."

"He's a Newfoundland mix, right?" Caden pushed Abel and Grey back and walked slowly toward the man. "Would you consider selling him? My omega here wants a dog," he said, rolling his eyes and nodding toward Grey.

The man shrugged, eyes roaming over Caden's designer clothes and shoes. "Eight hundred," he said. "I won't take anything less."

Caden dug through his wallet. "I have five hundred and twenty on me. Will you take a check for the rest?"

"I guess so," the man said, trying to act casual. Grey tried not to glare at him. The large dog was curled up against the dumpster, trembling. His dark fur was matted and filthy, and Grey couldn't tell what color he was in the dark. "He's two years old and isn't fixed. He was supposed to be a fucking guard dog."

Caden handed him the money and wrote the check. Grey and Abel moved to the dog, cooing and petting him. He stood right up, pressing his head against Grey's belly, as if he were trying to hear the baby. Grey giggled, hugging the fluffy head.

The man ran straight to the pub, shoving his money in his pocket. Caden came over and watched them pamper the big ball of fluff. "I'll stop by an ATM tomorrow, Caden, and pay you back," Grey said. "This big fella is all mine."

"Consider this your Christmas present," Caden said, finally managing a small smile.

CHAPTER 9

"You're sure you don't mind sitting with me?" Grey sat in the window seat of Harper's bedroom. He had staked an obvious claim on it, building a nest of pillows and quilts. His feet were propped up, Tiny in his lap.

Opal and Butterball were curled up together on the padded seat at his omega's feet. A clean, trimmed, and brushed Chewy lay beside them on the floor, snoring. He was a beautiful, shaggy brown with a cream colored chest.

"Of course, I don't mind," Harper said. "I know you're worried."

Harper loved that Grey wanted him there. Fuck, he was happy as hell that his omega was taking over his bedroom. More and more of Grey's things had found their way to his room. Cindy Bear now had a permanent perch amongst the pillows on his window seat.

Grey's phone rang, and he quickly put it on speakerphone. "Greyson Bishop."

"Hi, Grey. This is Delwick. I'll not try to take up too much of your time."

"It's not a problem, sir," Grey said, cringing. "It's good to hear from you."

"This situation has been a pain in the ass for me, so I know it's been even worse for you. I'm sorry for that. Now, I wanted to apologize to you about this whole situation. Lane was in a position of power, and he abused it. You got caught in the crosshairs, and that's unacceptable. I am truly sorry this happened under my watch."

"I understand, sir," Grey said. "Lane was very persuasive and fooled a lot of people."

"That he did," Delwick said wryly. "When we investigated, we found out that he wasn't just stealing work from you, but from all his subordinates in the department. He also stole money from petty cash and is being investigated for discrimination and sexual harassment."

"Oh dear."

"Like I said, it's been a pain in the ass. It's worth it though. We'll have a better company for it."

"Delwick's has a good reputation and a strong client base," Grey said, nodding enthusiastically. "It'll survive."

"It will, and we're happy to have you with us. I reviewed all the websites you've designed since you've been here, and let me just say, they are amazing. You have a real talent, young man, and I look forward to seeing where you go."

Grey looked at Harper in disbelief, but he just grinned. He knew how talented his omega was. Grey just had to figure it out. "Thank you, sir," Grey said. "I really appreciate it. I love working for Delwick's."

"Well, after reviewing everything, I will be giving raises to the whole team, reflecting their actual work. Each of you were far more productive than it appeared, so expect an e-mail from payroll. Also, for you specifically, I will be rewarding you for the award your site won. The money originally went to Lane, but it's yours. I'll be interviewing for Lane's position this week and hope to have someone in as early as next week. Grey, we really are happy to have you with us, and I promise I will keep a better eye on my employees. I never want anyone to feel threatened or bullied."

"Thank you, Mr. Delwick."

"One more thing. I know you start maternity leave in two weeks, but I want you to go ahead and take an extra two weeks, starting now. This has been stressful for you, and I'd hate to think of it hurting you or the baby. You just finished a project too, so the timing is perfect."

"Thank you, sir. I just moved so that would give me some extra time to settle in."

"Excellent! Make sure you file the change of address with Georgia. Enjoy your time."

The call ended, and Grey stared off into space. "I'm getting a raise, Mr. Delwick thinks my work is really good, and I won an award. Harper, can you believe this?"

Harper sat on the edge of the seat and gave Grey a

gentle hug. He wished he could give more, but he had to be patient. "You're a great website designer, Grey, so it's easy to believe. Speaking of designing, Aunt Anna has been bugging me to ask you about designing a site for Farm Fresh. We'll go through the company, but we want you to do it. Can you?"

Grey beamed. "I'm allowed to work independently. I just can't use the Delwick stamp." He pulled Harper into a hug, wiggling in his seat. "Consider the website a Christmas present from me to the family. I'll start working on it tonight."

"Absolutely not," Harper said. "You deserve to get paid for your work."

"No deal." Grey shook his head stubbornly. "It's a Christmas present, or I don't do it."

"I'll let you argue with Aunt Anna."

"Bring it!" A knock echoed from downstairs, and Opal started barking. "Opal, calm down," Grey said. "That's probably Abel. He's taking me to Abuela's for a few hours to knit. Grammy will be there too and is going to help me with my knitting. Will you help me up?"

Harper eagerly helped him to his feet, stealing a hug. Grey surprised him by leaning up and pressing his lips to Harper's. Harper froze for a second, then tightened his arms around his omega and pulled him close, pressing in and deepening the kiss. Grey's lips were warm and soft, parting easily for Harper's tongue. He'd never tasted anything so good, never felt so light and full of fire. He pulled back, panting, and enjoyed the sight of Grey's dazed eyes.

"Have a good time, Grey," Harper said softly, mentally cursing his hard dick. Now wasn't the time. "Gramps and Dad are coming by to paint the nursery."

"Thank you so much," Grey said, eyes luminous. "I'll be back in a little while with a present. Hopefully."

Harper and the beasts walked him to the door and waved him and Abel goodbye. As they pulled out, Gramps's truck pulled in. Harper's grandfather was a big man, tall with wide shoulders. He was in his sixties, but he still looked like he could climb mountains and slay dragons.

"Harper," Gramps said, nodding to him, then bending to pet Chewy. "How's Grey doing?"

"He's doing well. The doctor showed us the baby. Come on, I'll show you." He grabbed his arm and pulled him to the kitchen, Chewy, Butterball, and Opal following close on their heels. Harper pointed to the pictures on the fridge. "Isn't he beautiful?" Harper traced his son's little nose.

"Your boy looks good," Gramps said, throwing an arm around him. "You all decided on a name?"

"Grey hasn't said anything, but I think he'll name him Rue, after his brother."

"That sounds just right," Gramps said. "How about we get started on that nursery?"

"Yes," Harper said, running up the stairs. "Grey and I decided to go with yellow and white for the nursery. I have the crib made, but it still needs the bedding added. I've started on a rocker for Grey too. He has an old chair that belonged to his great-grandmother. I want to fix it up too, but it's not a rocker. He needs one right? To rock the baby?"

"Yep. We'll need a dresser, bookcase, toybox, and changing table before he comes too," Gramps mused. "What kind of wood you using?"

"Cedar. I bought a bunch from a friend in Tennessee."

"You mind some help or is this something you need to do yourself?"

"Your help is always welcome, Gramps. I want it to be family made." Chewy plopped in the doorway of the nursery, watching them curiously.

"I've got time, so I'll be by each morning until it's done. Your grandmother abandoned me for Ines anyway."

Harper laughed and opened the paint, stirring it. "I can see those two getting into a lot of trouble."

"How's Grey's ex handling things? I know he dumped Grey and ran, but has there been any other contact?"

"Grey said he signed over paternity rights months ago, and the guy did provide medical history on his family."

"That seems surprisingly nice of him."

"He was scared to death that Grey would sue him for child support, so he gave him everything he asked for."

"Asshole," Gramps said, grumbling.

"You two start without me?" Harper's dad was the younger version of his father. He came in with Opal in one arm and Butterball in the other. "These two couldn't make it up the stairs." He set them down and grabbed a roller. The two trouble-makers climbed over Chewy and ran for the hall, excited to explore the upstairs. "Harper gets to trim. His knees are younger."

"Yeah, yeah," Harper said, picking up the small brush.

"Son, while we work, there's something I need to tell you," Marco said reluctantly. "I wasn't going to bother with it, but your papa wanted me to."

"What's wrong?"

"Andrew has been causing a ruckus around town. Shawn overheard him making threats about Grey. Now, I don't think it's anything more than a bitter, spurned man, but Shawn said he was pretty nasty about it."

"What did he say?"

"That's the part I didn't want to mention. I know it'll upset you."

"Dad, tell me," Harper said, setting aside his brush.

"He said he was going to cut the baby out of Grey's belly and feed it to him."

"That's disgusting," Gramps said, scowling. He kept rolling the paint, steady and even. "Surely that boy knows what we'll do if he tries something like that."

"I don't know," Harper said, disturbed and pissed as hell. "Andrew has been really obsessive since we broke up, Gramps. I've had to delete my Facebook and Twitter accounts, and he's been banned from my website. Every time I see him in town, he yells at me, then tries to get me to sleep with him. It's not normal behavior."

"Damn, son. Despite what you said the other day, I didn't realize it was that bad." Marco set the brush down and pulled out his phone. "I'll talk to Ray and see if he can find anything out. You need to file a restraining order too."

"On what grounds? That he yells at me and flirts?"

"Psychological abuse, especially with his threats to Grey," Marco said. "I'll ask Shawn who else heard and start the process."

"I can do it, Dad."

"I know you can, but I want to help. You get to comfort our Grey, so I get to handle the other stuff." Harper rolled his eyes. His father loved to take care of everyone. "Get back to trimming."

"Yes, sir," he said, thinking about Andrew. No way would that fucker get near his omega.

"HARPER, ARE YOU HERE?" Grey walked into the kitchen. "Oh, there you are. I made you a present." Grey bounced on his feet, excited. Harper laughed at his sunshine.

Grey held out a wildly colorful scarf. At the top, it started out brown and cream, blocks of color alternating unevenly. Then, about a third of the way down, he'd switched to vertical hunter green and navy blue stripes, each stripe a different thickness. Those trailed off to light pink and hot pink vertical stripes. At the tail end of the extremely long scarf was a block of yellow with lopsided, neon green hearts. At each end was a line of deep purple fringe.

"See? I can knit, so you should throw out those tacky things that other omega made you. I'll make a bunch for you to replace them."

It took Harper a minute to realize he was talking about Ernie's knitted gifts. His cousin loved to knit and made sure every single family member, human or animal, had plenty of scarves and caps.

"You know that omega is Ernie, right? My cousin?"

Grey's mouth dropped open. "Hannah said some omega in town made them for you."

Harper laughed, falling back in his chair. "Well to be fair, Ernie is an omega, and he lives in town."

"That terrible girl," Grey said, pouting. "I did all that knitting for nothing."

"Why didn't you want me wearing anything made by another omega?" Harper watched Grey's face go from annoyed to embarrassed.

"No reason."

A slow smile crept across his face. "You were jealous." His omega was jealous. Between this and that kiss earlier, Harper knew they weren't just friends.

"Maybe," Grey said, avoiding his eyes.

Harper pulled his omega to him and tilted his face up. "I've been yours since we met months ago, Grey. There's absolutely no need to be jealous." He leaned down and kissed the omega's warm, sweet lips. He explored his mouth, slowly, hands slipping behind Grey, pulling him close.

"Harper," Grey moaned, making the alpha's heart beat faster. He lifted his omega, setting him on the counter and moving between his legs. Grey's pregnant belly pushed into his own flat one, reminding him to be gentle.

He pulled his mouth from Grey's and leaned his forehead against his omega's. They were both breathing hard, and Harper could feel Grey's erection. "Can I taste you?" he asked. "Please?"

Grey nodded, smile trembling. Harper fell to his knees, pulling Grey's stretchy maternity pants down his legs. He hummed in pleasure at the pair of silky, green underwear covering his omega's hard cock. He placed an open mouthed kiss against Grey's erection, reveling in the feel of hardness beneath silk. He licked along the shaft, moving slowly.

Grey gasped, then moaned, his knuckles white against the edge of the counter. Harper tugged and pulled his omega's dick from the panties, pumping hard. Fuck, what Grey's moans did to him. Not able to wait anymore, he licked him, root to tip, before taking him in his mouth. He worked him fast, up and down, soaking in every gasp, moan, and word of praise.

At the first taste of Grey's cum, he felt his own dick explode, soaking through his boxer briefs and jeans. He swallowed every bit of Grey he could, then stood, kissing his omega deeply, sharing his taste.

"The things you do to me, my sweet alpha," Grey said softly, cupping Harper's head and pulling him in for another kiss. "I'm sorry you didn't get to come."

Harper laughed, flushing. "I came in my pants. Ridiculous, right?"

Grey shook his head, kissing him again. "That's the hottest thing I've ever heard."

Eventually, Harper helped him straighten his panties and stretchy pants. He lifted him off the counter, setting him back on his feet.

Grey wobbled, then steadied. "That was amazing," he said. "I need to knit you things more often. I get a blowjob, and you get a gorgeous new scarf."

Harper held up the hideous thing. "I love it, and I can't wait to see what you create next."

Grey's shy smile was worth the lie. It was worth every teasing remark his cousins would make. It was worth everything.

CHAPTER 10

Grey carefully parked the Jeep outside Honey Buns and took a deep breath, trying to still his shaking hands. He'd made it down the mountain without dying in a ditch somewhere. He knew he needed to get used to driving on snow, but it scared him to death. After he regained his nerves, he walked along the sidewalk, heading toward the bakery.

"Watch out," someone yelled. Arms grabbed his shoulders from behind and pulled him against the nearest building just in time to miss the black truck flying past. It drove completely on the sidewalk, knocking down decorations and store signs. The truck zipped back to the road to avoid the iron street light, then turned a corner and was gone.

"Holy shit," Grey said, trembling. He'd almost died. That truck would have flattened him and the baby. He looked to his rescuer, eyes widening. "Thank you, Justin. Fuck. That was insane."

The other omega was stark white and shaking. "It

aimed straight for you," he said breathlessly. "It was on the road, then turned toward you. Jesus."

"Grey!" A young, blond woman flew out the door of the bakery. "Are you okay? That truck almost hit you." She pulled him into a tight hug.

"Zoe?"

"That's me," she said. "You two come in and sit down. Jules is calling the police right now. Did one of you get the license plate number?"

"I didn't," Grey said. The bakery was warm and cheerful. Christmas music played softly in the background, and the most wonderful scents filled the air.

"Me neither." Justin slid into the booth and put his face in his hands. "That was so close."

"I'll bring you some tea, Grey. Coffee, Justin?"

"Please."

Zoe walked away, and Grey watched Justin. "Thank you, Justin. I would have died, or at the least, lost my son."

"You're welcome," he said, scowling.

"I have to admit, I'm kind of surprised. I thought you hated Harper, so why would you help me?"

Justin looked at him in disbelief. "I do hate Harper, but I don't want anyone dead. What kind of person would be like that?"

"Harper's other ex, Andrew."

"Yeah. That man is definitely messed up."

"I know it's not really my business, but why do you hate Harper so much?"

Justin looked out the window, watching the snow

fall on the trashed sidewalk. "We dated for three years in high school. He cared, I know he did, but it was like pulling teeth with him. He wasn't like my friends' boyfriends. They couldn't keep their hands off their omega or girlfriend. It just made me feel…" He trailed off with a huff.

"Feel what?"

"Feel like I wasn't enough, that maybe there was something wrong with me. It had to be me, because everyone knows it's always the omega's fault. Plus, he's a Wilson."

"First, if anyone assumes it's the omega's fault, they're an idiot. Second, the Wilsons aren't perfect," Grey said. "No one is. They just tend to be loving and supportive."

"Most families aren't like that," Justin said, sadness filling his face.

"You mean, *your* family isn't like that."

"Yeah," Justin said. "My dad left us when I was ten, and we were poor, dirt poor. It was hard on Mom, so she started messing with pills. It got bad, and I didn't have anyone. Meanwhile, there's the Wilsons, and they're perfect. I wanted so badly for things to work out with Harper."

"Then it didn't."

"Everyone I knew thought it was my fault, myself included," he said. "No one knew he was demisexual until Andrew started sharing his business with anyone who would listen."

"Would it have made a difference? You know now, but you were really rude yesterday."

"I don't know. I'd like to think it would, but he's still a Wilson."

"Back to that?"

"They have money," Justin countered. "A lot of it."

"They work hard too. Harper's dad typically works twelve to fourteen hours, seven days a week. All the cousins work several hours a week in the store or on the farm on top of whatever their day job is. I think it's their favorite hobby."

Justin looked pissed. "They aren't the only hard-working people around here. Do you know how hard it is to find a job in this town? It's tiny, and there's hardly anything available. The Wilsons don't just survive like the rest of us, they fucking thrive. I'm a damn cashier at the grocery store."

"You're jealous? That's why you're still bitter about the breakup?"

Justin bowed his head, rubbing his hands over his short hair. "I'm fucking green with it. I try not to be, but it's so hard. I have to stay in town because of Mom. She's sick. I can't find any good work, since I don't have more than a GED."

"Hmm," Grey said, thinking about his new friends.

"Then I started dating Tanner, and he's amazing. I don't want to be some shitty, needy omega, you know?"

"Trust me. I understand," Grey said.

"I know I'm a dick every time I see Harper, but I can't seem to help myself."

"Here's what's going to happen. You're now my friend, whether you like it or not," Grey said. Justin tilted his head and watched Grey curiously. "In about twenty minutes, the others will get here. You are now an official member of the Hot Mess Club."

"Okay?" The man looked puzzled but accepting.

"Justin, are you alright?" Tanner and another police officer, Parker, sat at their table. Tanner wrapped Justin in his arms.

"He saved my life," Grey said, earning him a surprised look from both officers.

After Justin and Grey told the officers what had happened and all the details they could remember, Parker left to talk to the other customers and employees at the bakery. Tanner kissed Justin, then went outside to take pictures of the mess on the sidewalk.

Caden and Abel arrived together. Caden sat, while Abel glared at Justin. "What's he doing here?"

"He's the newest member of the Hot Mess Club," Grey answered, pointing to the empty seat. "Sit down."

"We have a name now? I love it," Abel said and sat beside Justin. "What happened to the sidewalk? Why's Tanner taking pictures?"

"Someone tried to run over Grey," Justin answered.

"The fuck say what?" Abel's gaze pinned Justin in his seat. "What do you mean? Someone tried to kill Grey?"

Justin explained what happened, again, and the four men stared at one another for a moment. Grey's pulse was still too fast, and he knew he was pale and shaking. He'd imagined death a thousand times, but he couldn't bear the thought of losing the baby or leaving Harper.

"The Hot Mess Club just got dangerous," Abel said. "Who do you think it was? Andrew maybe?"

"I don't know," Grey said, thinking of the latest threatening texts from Lane. "I don't want to think about it. Let's get moving. Who are we going to work on first?"

"Drinks first," Abel said, waving Zoe over.

"Why wasn't I invited to lunch," Zoe said, frowning. "I didn't know you were friends with Grey already." She glared at Abel, then turned to Caden. "Why didn't anyone say you were in town?"

"Because they don't know," Caden answered matter-of-factly. He took a notebook and pen out of his briefcase. "I'll have a large coffee, black."

"Seriously? I'm just dismissed?"

Grey couldn't help but giggle at her look of disbelief. "You aren't a hot mess, so you can't be in our club. Sorry."

She looked baffled, then gave up. "Whatever, you weirdos. What other drinks do you want? You get tea again, sweetheart," she said, patting Grey's belly.

"Doughnuts too?" Harper and Ines had refused to bring him doughnuts. Jerks.

Zoe gave him a soft smile. "Anything you want, Grey."

Once their drinks arrived, along with a plate of doughnuts and a plate of cinnamon rolls and Danishes, it was time to get to work.

"Wait," Caden said. "We need to know Justin's issues before we start. The more information we have, the better."

The three men turned to look at Justin. He sighed and took a sip of his coffee. "I have a shitty job and a pill-addicted mother. I love Tanner but don't want to be a burden on him."

"He wants to make more money so that he can support himself," Grey added. "He also needs to work on his self-image, like me, and his jealousy." He glared at Justin. "There's no need to take our unhappiness out on other people."

"Ugh," Justin said, rolling his eyes. "I know. I know."

"What kind of job do you want," Caden asked.

"I don't care," Justin said. "I only have my GED, so my boss won't promote me to management. I could do it though. I'm super organized and really good with numbers."

"I've been thinking of something since we talked last time," Caden said. "It might solve both Abel and Justin's problems. Plus, it would be good for the town."

"Does it involve the Irish Rose?" Grey had been doing his own thinking.

Caden nodded. "Yes. I checked, and it has been for sale for two years now. The owner wants fifty thousand for the whole thing. It even has an apartment over the pub."

"Eww," Abel said. "Who would want to own it?"

"You and Justin," Grey said, laughing at their looks of disgust.

"That place is a complete dive," Justin said.

"It is," Caden said. "But it could be so much better. Imagine a small, clean, and cozy pub serving locally crafted beer and good pub food. As it is now, there's no competition in town, so they get plenty of business. What if it was actually good?"

"It'd get a ton of business," Justin said, face filling with hope.

"I could brew my beer?" Abel sat up straight, eyes full of confidence. "It's good. I swear. I've already created six different recipes."

"I could so manage it," Justin said. "Maybe if I made enough, I could take some online business classes too."

"It would need a lot of work to get started," Grey said, thinking back to the filthy dump.

Justin's shoulders drooped. "I don't know what I'm thinking. There's no way I could contribute anything to buying and fixing it up."

"I don't know," Grey said, starting on his third doughnut. "It seems like you two could draft an agreement so part of your pay goes toward the purchase or something like that. I bet Elijah could make a kickass plan for you two."

"He could," Abel said excitedly, pulling his phone out and typing frantically. Everyone took a minute to eat some of the pastries and think over the plan.

Abel's phone chimed. "Okay, he says he'll do it. He also says I have the money to purchase the store outright and fix it up. It'll take a chunk out of what he's saved for me from the family investments, but that's what it's for, right?" He looked both scared and excited all at once.

"I'll make such an awesome website for you guys," Grey said, bouncing. He grabbed the last doughnut.

"I seriously can't wait to get started," Justin said. "I

can work during the day. I usually have the night shift at the grocery store."

"No," Caden said. "You both will need to devote as much time as possible toward the pub. Elijah has likely counted your salaries as part of his estimate for the renovation costs."

"Oh, my god, Justin," Abel said. "We need to get to work. We need to get the pub up and running, and I need to find somewhere to brew. Oh, my god."

Grey laughed and grabbed a Danish, since the doughnuts were gone. "You said there was an apartment above it too, Caden?"

"Yes, and it could likely be made into two if you both wanted to live there," Caden said.

"I would love to get out of Mom's trailer. I need to be close to her, but Lord knows, I don't need to be *that* close to her."

"We can keep it as one apartment," Abel said. "I'm not horribly unhappy at home and when I find somewhere to brew, I'll stay close to it. Plus, you never know. Tanner may move in with you, Justin." He smiled slyly at the other omega.

Justin blushed. "He might," he said and shrugged, failing at nonchalance. He couldn't keep the grin from his face.

"What about you two?" Justin looked between Grey and Caden. "Abel and I have a solution now, but what about you all?"

"Cain and my parents will be in town at Christmas. I'll tell them then."

"Tell them what?" Justin asked.

"That I'm going to be a romance novelist, not a lawyer."

"Okay," Justin said, drawing the word out. Grey kicked him and glared. He shook his head and smiled. "Good for you, man."

"We'll be there," Grey said, nodding firmly.

"Uh, you and Abel maybe," Justin said uncertainly.

"You too, Justin," Abel said. "Once you're in the Hot Mess Club, you're in it."

"We'll stand with you, Caden. It'll be alright," Grey said and handed the alpha a cinnamon roll.

"Grey? What about you?" Abel's eyes grew sad. "How can we help you deal with things?"

He drank his tea for a moment. "Mom loved Christmas, and she loved to cook. She taught me all of the family recipes."

"You can cook?" Abel sounded shocked.

"I can, but I don't. I'm fine heating up a casserole or making toast, but I stopped doing anything else."

"I take it your mom isn't around anymore?" Justin watched him carefully.

"No, my family died a while ago," Grey made himself say. "Every Christmas, Mom and I would cook goodies for everyone in the neighborhood. We'd decorate the house and bake. Then, we'd fill up cute tins and hand them out. Her family recipe box is packed in my blue crate. Tomorrow, I'm going to take it out and make cookies and decorate the house. I haven't decorated for Christmas since they died."

"That sounds like a good first step," Caden said. "What time do you want us to come by?"

"I don't work tomorrow," Justin said.

"I have all day off tomorrow too," Abel said. "Would ten be alright with you? We can go get a tree too. Harper is lazy about decorating for Christmas, so I know he has nothing up."

Tears filled Grey's eyes. He sniffed, trying to hold them back. "I'd like that."

"Grey!" Harper's panicked voice cut through the air. "Sunshine, are you alright? Zoe called and told us what happened."

Grey looked up, and Harper was there. His strong, sweet alpha. An older man that Grey assumed was Gramps stood beside him, wearing a matching worried expression. The two men looked just alike except for their ages.

"You aren't hurt, are you?" Gramps asked.

"I'm fine, guys," he said, getting up and settling into his man's arms. After a minute, he moved to Gramps, and the older man cuddled him close. "Justin saved me and the baby. He's my friend now." Grey nudged Justin with his foot, giving him a look.

Justin cringed. "Hi, Harper. I apologize for being a douche. I realize my issues with our breakup are *my* issues. You didn't do anything wrong, and I'm sorry if I made you feel bad about yourself. You're a great guy, and we just lacked communication and maturity."

Harper and Gramps stared at the man, mouths hanging open. Abel's chuckles turned into belly laughs. Grey tried to smother his own laughter, knowing this was an important moment for Harper and Justin both.

"Did you go to therapy since yesterday? If so, keep going," Harper said.

"Harper! That was rude," Grey said. Harper pulled him away from Gramps and back into his arms.

"Well, it's kind of true, though," Justin said. "I guess the Hot Mess Club is kind of like therapy."

"Yeah, but without the professionalism," Abel managed to wheeze between laughs.

"I'm happy that we're okay, Justin," Harper said. He tilted Grey's face up. "Is that powder sugar on your face? Have you been eating doughnuts for dinner again?"

"No," Grey said, shaking his head. "Justin ate all of them."

Justin looked at the empty plate. "Yes. I ate all thirteen doughnuts myself, then splattered powder sugar on Grey's face, so I wouldn't look like a pig."

"Sure," Harper said, dropping a kiss on Grey's head. "By the way, what the hell is the Hot Mess Club?"

CHAPTER 11

*H*arper watched Grey from the doorway. His omega stood in the kitchen, wearing his fox ears hat. A plate of pancakes waited for him on the table, and he held his belly. "Pancakes are the very best," he sang to his belly, swaying back and forth. "We'll eat them up, bite by bite. Look at all this deliciousness. Baby boy is truly blessed."

Harper grinned and slipped behind him, wrapping Grey in his arms. His hands rested on top of Grey's, covering the baby. He nuzzled his neck and placed little kisses along the side. Grey leaned back against him, still humming and swaying.

"Do you want some breakfast?" Grey turned and wrapped his arms around Harper's neck.

"I ate earlier. Gramps should be here any second," Harper said. "We're going to start on the changing table today. What are you doing? That's a lot of ingredients there on the counter."

"My friends are coming over to help me decorate the tree and do some baking."

Grey's voice cracked on the last word, and Harper gave him a soft kiss. "What's wrong, sunshine?"

"I still have to get Mom's recipe box out of the blue crate," Grey said. "It's harder than I thought it'd be."

"Come on," Harper said, starting toward the stairs. "Bring your breakfast with you."

Grey hustled behind him. "Don't forget Opal and Butterball," he said. "They can't do the stairs." He started slowly up the stairs, taking bites of pancake as he went.

Harper carried the two boogers with him, staying right behind Grey in case he fell back. Tiny took each step with Grey, watching him just as closely, and Chewy waited for them at the top of the stairs. *We are pet poor,* Harper thought with a smile. They made it to Grey's room, half a plate of pancakes shorter. Harper pulled the blue box out and set it gently on Grey's bed. Chewy jumped up on the bed and settled in with a drawn out sigh.

"Harper?" Grey said from the window seat, Tiny curled at his side while Butterball and Opal sat at Harper's feet, watching him eat. "We aren't just friends, are we?"

Harper went still and shivered. Finally. "No. We're not just friends," he answered his omega. "We're meant to be more than that."

"You could want someone like me? I'm huge, Harper."

Harper sat next to him, wrapping an arm around

him. "You're beautiful, Grey. I call you my sunshine, because that's what you are. You sparkle and shine every day, and your smile is just about the most beautiful thing I've ever seen. Plus, you're sexy as hell. Have you already forgotten yesterday? I've wanted you a long time now." He kissed his head. "Do you think you could want someone like me?"

"You mean someone who's handsome, sweet, kind, patient, and sexy? Yes, I could." Grey kissed his cheek. "You're a demisexual, not a mass murderer. You and I aren't you and Justin. I don't have some fantasy of us fucking 24/7."

"We could try it," Harper said. "I've been imagining it for over a month now."

Grey gave him a look of devastation. "You have to go and say that right now? Gramps will be here soon and so will my friends. That's just not fair."

Harper chuckled, then stood, moving back to the blue box. He took off the lid and was greeted with three pictures in cheap frames. Grey got his silly and joyous smile from his mom. She was blond and pleasantly plump, smiling and laughing. Grey's coloring came from his father. The man was slight, with tan skin and brown and gold hair. His eyes sparkled with mischief even though he smiled shyly. Grey's brother wasn't little. He was broad shouldered, well-muscled, and blond, dressed in a football jersey. His smile was somehow both confident and sweet.

Harper had to blink back his tears. Their pictures didn't belong in cheap, poorly made frames. They didn't belong in a box. He took them out, setting them aside. Grey averted his eyes, focusing on his pancakes. Harper dug into the box, pushing past a familiar jersey, jewelry tins, and leather-bound journals until he found a large, mostly broken, wooden box of little recipe cards, loosely held together with a scarf. He closed the crate and sat beside Grey again.

Gramps stood silently in the doorway, nodding to Harper when he saw him. He saw the pictures, frowning at the frames. He came in and gathered them up, likely thinking the same thing Harper had. They'd make better frames for Grey's family.

Harper handed over the box, taking his omega's empty plate. Grey wiped his eyes and untied the scarf, bringing it to his nose.

"What kind of goodies do you two like?" His voice was thick with tears, and he put the scarf behind him.

"We sure aren't picky," Gramps said, dislodging Tiny and sitting on Grey's other side. "Why don't you show us your favorites?"

Grey brushed his fingers over the tops of the cards. They were all different colors, some showing their age. "My favorite was my grandma's peanut butter balls. They're super easy to make and so good. Another really good one is Mom's peppermint chocolate biscotti. I loved those too." His fingers flew through the cards, quickly pulling out two. "See? If you put a recipe card in, you have to decorate it."

His grandmother's had little doodles of a snowman and a snowwoman. They hugged one another close. His mom's was decorated with star and heart stickers.

Gramps chuckled. "Did you put any in there?"

"Yes," he said, nodding excitedly and laughing. "I made peanut butter reindeer cookies. Rue always tried to steal them and eat them all." He pulled the card out. It had a little cartoon in the corner. Two boys chased each other, one of them clutching a plate of cookies, and the other one brandishing a rolling pin.

Gramps's laugh boomed through the room, and Harper couldn't help but join him. "I know we'll need some of those, sunshine."

"Okay. I'll make some bread too. I keep eating all of your papa's, because it's so good." Grey looked excited rather than sad. "I better get downstairs and start planning. The others will be here soon, I think." He kissed Harper's cheek and whispered, "I love you, Harper Wilson."

He stood quickly and gave Gramps a kiss too. He clutched the box and moved as fast as he could toward the door, peeking over his shoulder and smiling shyly.

Gramps watched him go with a smile. "That is one sweet omega you have there, my boy."

Harper touched his cheek, a smile splitting his face. "He said he loved me."

Gramps patted his back, shaking his head. "You'll be useless all day," he complained. "Come on. We need to make some pretty frames for his family pictures and a better box for his family's recipes. Did you finish those bookcases yesterday?"

Harper nodded. He had already had a few bookcases made to sell at the store, but he knew his omega needed some to replace his cheap ones. He'd taken two of the finished ones and carved woodland animals along the borders. They'd reminded him of one of the children's books Grey had made and shared with him.

"Let's get them up in the living room. His stuff's coming today, right? Laurel went to Ines's today to help her unload her stuff."

"Yeah," he said. "They're dropping off her stuff first, then bringing Grey's here."

The two men left the house as Carter's work van pulled up. The alpha got out and rushed to open the passenger door and help Elijah out.

"Hey, guys," Harper said. "I didn't expect you two today."

Three more vehicles pulled up and people poured out. His cousins Zoe, Janelle, Abel, and Noah waved, then ignored him, heading for the house. Caden, Justin, Tanner, and Mr. Bartley got out of another. The third held Aunt Anna, Uncle Barry, and their husbands, Uncle Jamie and Uncle Matt. Finally, Ines's car pulled up, and her and Grammy got out, waving as they headed to the house.

"So, Abel may have made a few calls," Elijah said sheepishly. "We want to be here for your omega."

"Hannah also told me I need to build some rabbit cages next to your chickens in the barn. Know anything about that?" Carter laughed at Harper's blank look. "Apparently, you and Grey are the proud new owners of fourteen Angora rabbits."

"What the hell? Are we getting new pets each day or something? Is this a weird Twelve Days of Christmas thing?"

"Come on, Carter," Gramps said, shaking with laughter. "I'll show you a good spot for them." Elijah tried to cover his giggles as he ran to the house.

"Son," Marco said, patting his back. Harper looked back, and, sure enough, his papa was hustling into the house. He'd waited four days. That was longer than Harper had expected him to. "You need help in the workshop? Everyone took the day off, except for Ernie and the kids in school. He couldn't find a sub."

Harper shook his head and shrugged. He did love his family, he reminded himself. "I really could use the help today. I wanted to get started on the changing table and the dresser. If you, me, and Gramps work fast, we could almost finish them all today."

"Let's get to it," Marco said. "First, though, I need to go hug your omega. Meet you there." He jogged toward the house, letting Tanner, Chewy, and Opal out at the door.

The police officer waved at Harper. Reaching him, he handed the puppy over. "Your omega said Opal and Chewy wanted to spend time with you guys today."

Harper rolled his eyes and took the puppy. More likely, Harper didn't want any accidents in the house while they had company. "Thanks."

"So, I was going to help Carter with the rabbit cages," Tanner said, walking beside him toward the barn. "I also wanted to update you on the case. Grey seems a little emotional today, so I didn't want to upset him."

"What did you find out?"

"We're treating it as attempted murder. Everyone

agrees that the truck turned and aimed straight for Grey. If my Justin hadn't been there, he'd be dead."

Harper closed his eyes and breathed deeply. His omega and son could have died. Zoe had told him, but hearing it from the police made it somehow more real. "Do you know who the driver was?"

"That's the problem. The truck had tinted windows and no tags. I have the feeling it was paid for with cash for the sole purpose of murdering your omega. I know that's a reach, but it's what I think. We're checking out places in the area that could have sold it, but if I'm right, then it's likely the person bought it from out of the area. I have some contacts in the closest towns checking it out."

"What about Andrew?"

"We talked with him, and he has an alibi. Not an ironclad one, but it's there. We're still treating him as a person of interest because of his threats. Your brother, three of his friends, and two of their parents heard him."

"What about his old supervisor, Lane?"

"Grey forwarded all the threats, and this guy is definitely in the running. We haven't been able to track him down yet."

"Thanks, Tanner," Harper said, worry tinting his voice. "I can't lose him."

"Considering how many people care about him, I don't think it will be hard to keep him in company until we get this figured out."

"That's true," Harper said, entering his workshop. Gramps had already started on some picture frames.

Harper headed to the cedar pile to start picking out likely pieces for the changing table. Chewy settled into a large dog bed in the corner, pinning Opal between his paws. He laid his big head on top of the puppy. Opal licked Chewy's nose and settled in to watch them work.

A few minutes later, his dad, Noah, Uncle Matt, and Uncle Jamie came in, each moving in to help. With a full day from all of them, they may be able to knock out most of the nursery. He may not have protected his omega, and maybe he couldn't figure out who'd tried to kill him, but he could take care of him in other ways for now. His house was full of family and friends. They weren't alone. They could do this together.

CHAPTER 12

"Next time you almost die, querido, you tell me," Abuela said. "Why do I need to keep reminding you that I love you? You're my sweet boy." She reached up and kissed his cheek while he rolled out the dough for his cookies.

"We all love you, Grey," Grammy said, kissing his other cheek. "No one threatens our family and gets away with it."

"Leave him alone, you two," Anna said, pushing them away. "Grey, my dearest Grey," she said. "Can we please, please, please make this recipe for cannelloni? I can't believe you have recipes from your Italian great-grandmother. You're getting a pasta maker for Christmas."

Grey smiled shyly at the bubbly woman. "It takes a while, but it's really good."

"We're doing it," Anna yelled and ran back to Abel and Elijah. The two omegas cheered.

"Greyson," Barry said from the door. "The movers

are here with your things. Caden and I will take care of it, alright? You just keep making those delicious-smelling cookies." Butterball stood beside him, head cocked, waiting for Grey's answer. She wore a little red and green Christmas sweater.

"Thanks, Uncle Barry. Just put everything in Harper's room. I'm moving in there tonight." Grey opened one of the oven doors on the double oven and took out the fresh pan of cookies. They needed to be decorated.

Every person in the kitchen catcalled and whistled, startling him and Tiny both. The large cat was basking in the bay window over the sink, between a small fern and a potted Aloe plant.

"That's just wonderful," Bennett said, hugging him tightly. "We love you so much."

Grey leaned into the man's hug, soaking up his affection.

A few minutes later, Barry ducked back in, Butterball at his heels. "Sweetie, are you sure you want to keep the IKEA furniture? Matt and Jamie brought in two new bookcases for you, and you'll be sharing Harper's bed."

Grey thought for a minute. The bed, bookcases, dresser, and desk were fairly new, but Harper did love making things. He looked around the kitchen. "Would anyone like three bookcases, a twin sized bed, a desk, and a dresser? They're in good shape, but Barry is right."

"If no one else wants them, I'll take them," Justin

said. "I'll need furniture for the apartment when it gets fixed up."

"Yes," Grey said happily. "That's perfect."

"We'll have them put in the barn for now," Barry said. "They'll be dry and out of the way." He hurried back out the door.

David Bartley grabbed the pan of peanut butter reindeer cookies. "I'll get these decorated, baby doll," he said. The man was amazing. He wore a bright red, chunky sweater, tight jeans, and heeled boots. His make-up was flawless.

Grey had tried to wear make-up once. It had been bad, very bad.

"Mr. Bartley, can I help do that too? Please?" Zoe bounced on her feet. "I love decorating cookies, and Grey's design is so cute."

"Of course you can," he said. "But only if you all quit calling me Mr. Bartley. It makes me feel old."

"Will do, David," she said and sat with him at the table.

Grey shared an amused look with Bennett, then put the pan of hot cocoa cookies into the newly emptied oven. Now for the biscotti. "Bennett, do you want to help me with the biscotti mix?"

"Of course," he said, moving closer to his side.

Abuela moved to his other side. "Are you trying to replace me, mi corazón?"

"No," he said with a laugh. "In fact, I'm counting on you to make me tamales tonight. I know we'll have cannelloni, but I've been craving your tamales. Now that I'm cooking again, I need to learn some of your recipes to put in the box."

Ines sniffled. "I love you, querido. Nothing would make me happier."

"Abuela," he whispered. "Will you do me a favor?"

"Anything," she said.

"Will you unload the blue crate on my bed? I don't know if I can do it all at once, but I like the idea of Dad's journals and favorite books on the shelf and Mom's jewelry on our dresser."

"I'll do it now. Laurel and I are going to search for decorations anyway. We'll do it first." She kissed his cheek again, lingering. "I don't want to leave you," she said.

Grammy pulled the woman away, and the two went to hunt down Harper's Christmas decorations.

"She's a good woman," Bennett said. "I'm glad you have her."

"Me too," he said quietly. "She reminds me a lot of Mom. She was a fire cracker, so sweet but so feisty. I don't think I would have survived losing all of them without Abuela."

"I think you helped her, just as much as she helped you," Bennett said. "She needed someone to love and pamper. Maybe fate knew the two of you needed one another."

"I think so," Grey said, thinking of his mom. She would have adored Ines. The two would have been fast friends, just like Ines and Grammy. The pain was there as he thought of her, but it didn't hurt so much with

Bennett beside him and the others spread throughout the kitchen.

"Grey, do you want me to put your dolls in the living room too?" Caden poked his head into the kitchen.

He gasped as the others snickered. "They aren't dolls, Caden. They're collectables."

"Sure," he said, clearly not believing Grey. "In the living room?"

"Yes, please. I'll have Harper do another bookcase when he gets a chance."

"Put them on the top, Caden," Elijah said. "Puppies and babies like to chew on collectables. That's where my Star Wars figurines went."

"No, that was Carter," a man with a green Mohawk said from the doorway. "He likes to chew on things. It wasn't Hotdog, I swear."

"Juan," Elijah said happily, rushing over to hug the man. "Grey, this is our friend Juan. He's basically family now, so you'll see him around a lot. Is Ray here too?"

"He ran to hide in the barn. He'll be by to introduce himself at some point. I just came from there too. Matt finished up something, and I thought Grey might like to see it."

"What is it?" Grey followed Juan, gasping when he saw his great-grandmother's chair sitting near the fireplace. "It's beautiful!" Someone had smoothed out the old wood and applied a coat of clear stain. It glowed like new. The cushions on the seat and back had been redone in red plaid. It looked adorable. "This is just gorgeous." He couldn't believe it was the same chair.

"Harper had it started, but Matt finished it up," Barry said, carrying a box of books into the living room. "I have the cutest little ottoman at home that would match it perfectly. I'll get Ernie to stop and pick it up on the way out. You'll be all comfy with your feet propped up before you know it."

"You guys are amazing," Grey said, tears filling his eyes. He watched as his things mixed with Harper's. Their home was coming together.

SIX HOURS LATER, Grey was out in the snow, wrapped in Harper's arms as they looked at the house. Colorful lights wound around the rails of the porch and along the top of the house. Garland twisted around each porch post and a lovely wreath hung on the door. Grey could see the Christmas tree through the living room windows. It was huge and covered in ornaments, lights, and strands of beads. A Santa hat was perched atop it.

"It's beautiful, isn't it?" Harper settled his chin on Grey's head, humming a Christmas carol. "Let's get inside before we freeze."

"Gramps said a storm was supposed to pass through tomorrow. Will we get even more snow?" There was already three feet packed on the ground. It was pretty, but it was cold and a pain to walk through.

"Probably quite a bit."

Harper helped him up the stairs. Inside, the house

was covered in Christmas decorations. Grey strongly suspected it wasn't all Harper's stuff. Somehow, extra boxes had appeared in the house.

"It smells so damn good in here," Harper said.

"Come on, you two," Hannah said. "We're waiting on you to eat."

"I'm starving to death, Uncle Grey," Olive, Elijah's daughter, said, grabbing his hand. "Please hurry before I fade away." Her big brown eyes looked pitiful.

Grey laughed at her and followed the girls into the kitchen to make up a plate. Their family and friends spread throughout the house, sitting where they could, talking and laughing. They ate his great-grandmother's cannelloni and Abuela's tamales. Grey had begged Bennett to make lobster pie. It was Grey's new favorite thing in the world. They had already decimated most of Grey's baked goodies.

He sat in his great-grandmother's refurbished chair. It was a hell of a lot more comfortable than it had ever been when he was a kid. He sighed, propping his feet on the little red ottoman Ernie had picked up from Uncle Barry's house.

Butterball and Opal ran around the living room, excited to visit with all the people, while Tiny quickly disappeared upstairs, preferring his privacy. Chewy settled down beside Grey's chair, panting. Harper had sent another bookcase to the house, and all his books and Pops! figurines had a home. They mixed in with little carved, wooden forest animals and flowers. His alpha was a damn talented man.

His dad's journals were stacked neatly on the top

shelf of one of the beautifully carved bookcases, and his family's pictures were spread out with the knickknacks. Their new frames were the perfect highlight for his loved ones. Seeing them, having them mixed with his and Harper's things, gave him a strange sense of peace. His past was starting to settle in, and it wasn't a bad feeling.

"Grey, I love your children's books," Elijah said, settling down on the couch. "Why aren't they published?"

Grey shrugged, shoving lobster pie in his mouth. He swallowed. "I never tried to get them published. They're just for fun."

"Would you care if I showed them to some people?"

"I guess not," he said. "I think they're cute, but that's just me."

"And me," Harper said from the floor in front of the fire.

"Me too," Elijah and Olive said at the same time, giggling together.

"Okay then," Grey said with a laugh. "You've convinced me."

"Good," Elijah said, all smug and happy.

"Hey everyone," Abel yelled. "It's time." He was piled down with wrapped boxes and gift bags. Caden and Justin followed behind him, weighed down with their own stacks of gifts. "Grey, we wanted to throw you a baby shower, and this seemed like the perfect time. There's good food, we're all here, and we have gifts."

"You all didn't have to do that," Grey said, astonished. "You've only known me for a week or so."

"We've known you longer than that," Grammy said from Gramps' lap. "Harper wouldn't stop talking about you ever since the two of you met."

"Grammy," Harper said, blushing. Grey laughed at his sweet alpha.

"Let's get these presents opened," Justin said. "Mine first." He handed Grey a blue and silver striped gift bag. "This is from Tanner and me."

"Thanks, Justin," Grey said and handed his empty plate to Harper. He dug through the paper and pulled out a fox shaped night light. "This is so cute," he said, tears welling. "I love it."

Justin grinned and shrugged, handing him the next present. After a million gifts later, Harper and Grey had a ton of baby clothes of differing sizes, knitted baby mittens, beanies, a knitted stuffed fox, handmade rattles and set of wooden ABC blocks, a car seat, a stroller, and a ton of classic kid's books.

"This one was my favorite when I was a baby," Olive said, handing him a worn copy of Emily Winfield Martin's *The Day Dreamers*.

"Sweetie, don't you want to save it for your little brother or sister," Grey asked, sending a questioning look to Elijah, but he just shrugged and grinned.

"No. I want your baby to have it," she said. "He's my cousin, and I'll read with him lots and lots."

"Thank you," he said, pulling her in for a hug.

"We have one more," Ines said. Her and Grammy stood in front of him, holding Rue's jersey. He felt a jerk of pain, but he didn't shy away from it. Not this time. "We want to take your brother's jersey and make a blanket for the baby. Can we do that, querida?"

He nodded, speechless.

"We'll take good care of it," Grammy said, kissing his forehead.

~

"HARPER," Grey said, sitting in their bed, a book on his belly. Their friends and family had gone, and the house was quiet again. Opal and Buttercup were curled on their bed, and Chewy slept in the window seat, head balanced on Cindy Bear. Tiny was curled beside Grey, waiting for the two men to settle down so he could pick a spot to sleep.

Harper turned down the covers and climbed into bed. "Yes, sunshine?"

"When I was little, Dad used to read me his favorite book before bed. It became my favorite book, but I haven't looked at it since I was about twelve."

"Is that what you have there?"

"Yes," Grey said, holding the book up. "It's *The Little Prince* by Antoine de Saint- Exupéry."

"I don't think I've read it."

"Dad said that it was the book that taught him how to love. There's a part here that suits you and me."

Harper grinned. "Really?" He settled onto his side, reaching out and stroking Tiny's back. "Do tell."

"It's a conversation between the little Prince and a fox about taming people," Grey said and held the book up. "The fox explains to the Prince that to tame something is to *establish ties* with it."

"Okay," Harper said, smiling indulgently, baffled. "Like taming a horse? You have to establish a bond, get it to trust you."

"Yes. The fox says that at that moment, to the boy, the fox isn't anything special, just one fox among many. In return, to the fox, the Prince is also just one little boy, no one special. It's like that saying that there's plenty of fish in the sea, right? Anyway, if the Prince tames the fox, the fox will see him as a unique boy, with no one else like him in the world."

Harper frowned. "So, to be tamed is to see the person that tames you as someone special? Something unique?"

"Yes," Grey said. "It's the bond that does it, the time spent with each other, the words spoken, just like the time spent taming a horse, but with people."

"What happens with the Prince and the fox?"

"The Prince tames the fox, and then the fox tells him that if you tame someone, you become forever responsible for them."

"So, if you tame someone, they love you and need you, so you become responsible for them?" Harper sat up and scooted closer, lifting Tiny to the other side of the bed.

"Yes," Grey said solemnly. "You've tamed me, Harper. You aren't just some guy, and you're not just some friend. Or one man among many. You're my one and only. You have my heart now, so be careful with it, okay? You're responsible for it."

Harper's eyes were wet when he kissed him, and the salt from his tears mixed with his taste. His alpha cupped Grey's face, deepening the kiss, before slowly letting up. "You tamed me too, Grey. I never expected anyone to have the patience for me, but you did. Every conversation we had, every secret we shared, was you taming me. I love you, and I'll protect your heart with my life. You have mine too, but I know, with everything in me, that you'll treasure it."

CHAPTER 13

Harper pulled Grey to him, kissing him deeply. Heat spread through his body, making his dick hard as stone. Knowing that Grey felt as deeply for him as Harper did for his omega broke something in him. He couldn't, wouldn't, hold back anymore. They belonged together.

He slipped Grey's shirt up and off, baring his precious belly. He bent down and pressed small kisses over Grey's belly while his hand worked Grey's pants down his legs. He pumped Grey's cock, settling down to pleasure his man.

"Harper," Grey said with a moan. "I want you in me. Please?"

"Don't have to ask me twice," he said, stroking Grey one more time. "Uh, what's the best way to do this?"

Minutes later, Grey was on all fours, ass tilted in the air. Harper stretched him, dick lubed up and ready. He leaned over his omega, slipping in, groaning as he went. He licked a line up Grey's spine, sinking deep inside his omega. Harper started slow, easing in and out, but that didn't last long. Urged on by Grey's loud moans, he pounded hard and fast into him, gripping Grey's hips tightly in his hands.

Grey quickly came, his body tightening around Harper's cock. Harper thrust wildly, two more times, then poured into Grey with a loud shout. Panting, he buried his face against Grey's neck, placing small kisses along his sweaty skin. They settled in close to one another, Grey's back pressed tightly against Harper.

"I love you, sunshine," Harper said.

"I love you too, my sweet alpha." Grey's voice was soft and sleepy, and soon enough, soft little snores filled the air.

CHEWY'S BARKS WOKE HARPER. He sat up, looking over at the dog. He stood on the window seat, eyes fixed outside. Chewy growled deep and barked again. Opal joined in, though she couldn't see whatever Chewy did.

"What's wrong," Grey asked sleepily.

"I don't know," Harper said, moving to the window. "Fuck. Someone's out at the barn."

"One of our family?" Grey's words warmed Harper. The Wilsons were Grey's family now too.

"I don't think so," Harper said. "There's no reason for any of them to be out there." He watched the bent figure. The flood lights finally popped on when the person moved closer to the door. "He's trying to light a fire. Fuck. Grey, call the police."

Harper hurriedly dressed and ran down the stairs, grabbing his coat. Chewy followed, growling.

They dashed to the barn just as the person managed to get a fire started right inside the barn door. As the figure grew closer, Harper recognized him. Andrew glanced back when he heard them approaching. Eyes widening, he dropped the scrap wood he carried and took off at a run. Chewy went after him, darting in front of him. The large dog crouched low and growled at the man, and Andrew yelled, freezing in place.

Harper quickly kicked the wood away from the flames, and then dumped as much snow as he could on the small fire, but it still burned. He ran into the barn and quickly hooked up the hose he used to water the horses. His two boys were restless, moving about their stalls. Harper turned the water on and set up a steady stream on the fire.

"Harper," Parker said from the door. "Tanner has Andrew in custody. I'm so sorry we didn't get here earlier." The man started dumping snow on the fire to help. "We were following Andrew, and he gave us the slip, coming straight here. We were already on our way when Tanner got a call from Justin. Your omega called the police, then sent out a group text. Don't be surprised when your whole damn family shows up."

The fire was dwindling, finally, and Harper breathed a sigh of relief, keeping the water pouring. "Can you let the boys out? They hate the snow, but they'll appreciate being away from the fire."

"Will do," Parker said and rushed to their stalls.

"Harper, are you alright?" Grey waddled into the barn.

"We're fine, sunshine," he said as the last of the flames went out. "Luckily, Andrew didn't use gasoline or anything."

"Why did he do this?" Grey asked. "He would have killed the horses and chickens, not to mention ruining the workshop."

"Harper, Grey, are you two alright?" Bennett ran in, tears streaming down his face. "My boys," he said, pulling them into a hug. "Where's that fucker at?"

"Parker and Tanner are loading him in the car now, baby," Marco said. "Damn, Bennett. I didn't know you could run that fast."

"Someone tried to hurt my boys," Bennett said, growling.

"Rein it in there, Papa," Harper said. The fire's out, the animals are fine, and Grey and I aren't hurt."

Tanner slipped in, worry on his face. "There is something wrong with that man," he said. "Seriously, I think he has a mental disorder. We're taking him straight to the hospital."

"What's wrong with him?" Grey asked, cuddled into Harper's side.

"He's rambling about Harper being his. He thought that he needed to burn the barn down and blame it on Grey. Then Harper would leave Grey and come running to him."

"What the hell?" Marco said.

"That's what I mean," Tanner said. "There really is something wrong with him."

"Has he said anything about trying to run over Grey?" Bennett asked.

"Nothing," Tanner said. "Right now, he's pretty out of it. We're going to do a drug test too, but I really think it's something mental."

"We'll let the doctors figure it out," Harper said. "Papa, will you help Grey back inside? Dad and I will look around the barn. Make sure nothing else is out of place."

"Of course," Bennett said. "Come on, sweetie." The two omegas left, Chewy walking protectively at their sides.

They found two more spots set up to light. One next to the chicken run and the other right outside his workshop.

"I'm glad you have Chewy and those flood lights," Marco said.

"Me too," Harper said, shaking his head.

"Get to bed, son. Your papa and I are staying the night. You need some rest." Marco wrapped his arm around Harper's shoulders.

"Thanks, Dad," he said, leaning into his dad's side. A few minutes later, he crawled into bed and curled around Grey, quickly falling asleep.

Harper slept in the next morning. When he finally woke up, Tiny was balled up next to his head, purring. His omega was already awake and gone, but his scent was still in the air. Harper sighed happily, petting Tiny. He got up and stretched. After dressing, he went downstairs and found his omega in his chair next to the fire, feet propped up, watching the television.

Chewy sat on his haunches, head propped on Grey's belly, while Opal and Butterball chased each other, running off their energy.

Grey looked up, smiling when he saw him. "Hey, sweetness. Papa, Grammy, and Abuela are in the kitchen making breakfast. Gramps and Dad are already out in the workshop. I don't think they want to leave us alone."

"If we get free food and help in the workshop out of it, I guess it's okay," Harper said, leaning down to kiss Grey. His phone rang, and he checked the screen. "Hey, Tanner," he said, moving from the living room. He didn't see any sense in stressing Grey out with news of Andrew.

"Hey. I just wanted to update you. Come to find out, Andrew was recently diagnosed with schizophrenia. His family has been contacted, and the doctor the department works with is suggesting medication and rehabilitation. Andrew doesn't remember anything about renting a car to run over Grey, but we can't rule it out. Right now, he isn't a reliable source of information, even assuming he's being honest."

"I hope it's over now. Have you managed to figure out where Lane is?"

"No, and that worries me," he said. "I want to say it's over now, that we got the right guy, and you don't have to worry anymore, but honestly, I can't. Andrew very well could have tried to kill Grey, but it's strange that no one knows where his ex-boss is. Keep your eyes open, and we'll work double time on this, okay?"

"Yeah. Thanks for being honest, Tanner."

"No problem. My omega adores Grey. Crazy right?"

"Yeah," Harper said with a laugh. "They're supposed to be arch-enemies." Bennett ran out of the kitchen, hands covering his mouth. "Uh, I got to go. Thanks again, Tanner."

He raced to the bathroom door and heard retching. "Papa, are you okay?" He pushed the door open and rushed to Bennett's side. "Papa?"

Bennett gave him a wane smile, hugging the toilet. "Congratulations. You're getting another sibling."

"Yes," Grey cheered from the doorway. "I'm sad about the morning sickness—I hated it—but I'm so happy for you. You're such a good father. Your newest addition will be the luckiest baby in the world."

"Oh, sweetie," Bennett said from the floor. "You and Harper will make wonderful parents. I just know it."

Harper helped his papa up, and he and Grey gave him some privacy.

"Grey," Harper said, pulling his omega to him. "The baby will be here in a few weeks."

"Yes, he will."

"Will he be a Bishop or a Wilson?"

"What are you asking?"

"Are you going to stay a Bishop, or do you want to become a Wilson?"

"Are you asking me to marry you, sweet alpha?" Grey's silly, joyful smile warmed Harper's heart.

"Yeah. I am. I know it's fast, but I want the baby to be a Wilson. I want you to be a Wilson."

"Of course, I'll marry you," Grey said. "I already

planned on the baby being named Rupert Bishop Wilson, so this means less paperwork."

"It won't be less paperwork," Bennett said, coming from the bathroom. "But it will be amazing. I'll take care of everything. We can do it right before the festival next week."

"I like that idea," Grey said. "The festival can be like our reception, but only our friends and family will know, so the spotlight won't be on us."

Harper had no idea what he meant, but he knew his omega wanted to legalize their bond. That was all he really needed to know.

CHAPTER 14

A week later, Grey held an Angora rabbit in his arms, scratching the big boy's fuzzy ear, while Hannah collected the rabbit poop. Their bunnies were adorable, and Grey, Chewy, Butterball, and Opal spent as much time as possible in the barn visiting them. Tiny preferred the warmth and privacy of the house.

"Back to bed, Mr. Darcy," Grey said, placing the bunny back into his rabbit condo. He moved to the next and took out a new rabbit. "How are you today, Heathcliff?" The huge, grey rabbit wiggled his nose. "I'm glad to hear it."

"Do you talk to the rabbits every day?" Hannah asked, laughter in her voice.

"Of course," he said. "Every morning, I take them out for a cuddle and a few words. Then in the evening, they need another cuddle and some pampering. I brush their hair, and they get to visit with Dumpling and Boon. Those two are secret bunny lovers."

Hannah hooted. "I can't wait to tell Doc. He was worried that you'd regret taking them on."

"Did I miss Hamlet's turn?" Elijah ran in, going right to the next rabbit. "How's my pretty boy?" Hannah laughed harder. "What's wrong with her?"

"Who knows? Hi, Juliet," he said, taking out the large, white, and pregnant female. "Do you want to say hello to your best friend this morning? Hannah, pick up Opal, please. One day, I'll be able to bend over."

Hannah picked up the puppy, and Opal and Juliet bumped noses. "Okay, that might be the cutest thing I've ever seen," she said.

"Sunshine," Harper said, finishing with the chickens. "Aren't you supposed to be getting ready for the wedding?"

"I have to take care of my babies first," he said.

Harper shook his head, then checked on his ponies. They would be working hard today, pulling the sled at the winter festival. Boon was visiting with Elijah and Hamlet. Grey watched his alpha, following his every movement. That was his man, his sweet alpha. Yummy.

"Eww," Hannah said. "Stop looking at him like that. It's disgusting."

"I can't help it," Grey said. "Just avert your eyes."

"The wool from these rabbits will be perfect for my next batch of yarn," Ernie said, coming in with Abel and Zoe. "They're almost ready to harvest, right?"

"About another week or so," Grey said. "Elijah and Hany are going to help Harper and me when it's time."

"That baby may come first," Abel said. "He's sitting kind of low, isn't he?"

"I have two more weeks," Grey said stubbornly, stomping his feet.

"Okay," Abel said. "I've heard babies always come when it's convenient for the parent."

Elijah snickered. "Grey, we can finish taking care of the bunnies. You should go get ready."

"Come on," Abel said, pulling his arm. "Put the bunny down, so we can fix you up."

"We?"

"Mr. Bartley is waiting for us in your room."

Grey gasped. "He'll make me pretty?"

"Sunshine, you're always pretty," Harper said, picking up Butterball and scratching her ear.

Grey gave him a kiss. His sweet alpha was the very best.

"Let's go," Abel said, pulling him along. "No kissy, kissy."

Chewy followed them. The gentle dog had become very protective of the household since the fire. He didn't growl and bite, but he always stood guard. Grey stroked his furry, brown head as they walked to the house. Bennett, Grammy, and Ines were cooking up a storm. They planned on feeding everyone before they headed to the festival.

The large living room was transformed into the perfect wedding venue. Harper and Gramps's handmade driftwood arbor stood in front of the windows, and chairs were arranged in rows, awaiting guests. Janelle's floral creations were spread out on every surface, adding color to the room.

At the moment, Janelle, Aunt Anna, Uncle Barry,

and their spouses, were setting up the festival early, so they could enjoy the wedding. Farm Fresh hosted the festival every year, so it was quite a bit of work. Luckily, the Wilsons were a large family, and the town always loved helping.

"Wait, Abel," Grey said, pausing in the upstairs hallway. "Look at the nursery. It's finally finished."

He opened the door and showed off his sweet alpha's hard work. The walls were a warm yellow with white trim. The crib was smooth and shiny with vines carved up the legs. The blanket draped on the rails was a tiny quilt, piecing together his brother's yellow and blue jersey, a gift from Grammy and Ines. They had made a little swaddling blanket out the left over pieces.

The rocking chair sat in the corner with a small ottoman. The arms were decorated with mama and baby bears. Cindy Bear perched in the seat, waiting to comfort a new generation. The rest of the furniture was just as intricate and beautiful, decorated with animals and forest scenes. The bookcase was full of children books, including his own and his dad's copy of *The Little Prince*. The large stuffed alligator with the Santa hat sat atop it. It was a beautiful room made with love. Grey wiped at his tears.

"It's beautiful, Grey." Abel wiped his own tears. "I'm so happy Harper found you, that you found each other. Your family is stunning, and little Rue will only make it even better."

"Thanks," Grey said. "How's the pub project going?"

"We've drawn up the contract between Justin and me. His share of the profits will go toward his portion until it's paid off. He'll still draw a nice salary though. We've also talked to the owner and are in the process of buying it."

"I can't wait until it's yours. You and Justin are going to make it amazing." They entered the bedroom, and David looked up from his makeup box.

"Finally," he said. "I wondered when you two would get here."

The older man looked beautiful, as usual. His short dark hair was styled, and his makeup flawless. He wore a pale pink silk blouse that hung perfectly from his narrow frame. His grey leggings molded to his body, and his heeled boots were the perfect addition to his outfit. He looked delicate and gorgeous.

Grey sat in the chair he'd pointed to and watched the man peruse his makeup line up. "Are you seeing anyone, David?"

He peeked over his shoulder and waggled his brows. "Are you asking? This is a bit sudden, doll face, and I think Harper might object."

Abel laughed. "He really would."

"You know what I mean," Grey said, poking him.

David began applying some kind of base or foundation, something, to his face. "I'm not lucky in love, boyos. My dates usually turn into really good friends or complete jerks."

"Have you ever been in love?" Abel ran his hands over the silk, cream colored shirt that Grey would wear.

"Once," he said softly, spreading a powder across

Grey's face. "I met my soulmate, but he was happily married with two kids and one on the way."

"That's not fair," Abel said. "Did he love you too?"

"Not the way I needed him too. He became my best friend, and I hid how I felt for a long time."

"What happened?" Grey hated the thought of David hurting. He was such a sweet and gentle man.

"I couldn't do it anymore. Work made me act and dress a certain way. Then, when I wasn't at work, I was at their house. I couldn't possibly find anyone else, not when he was right there every day." He grabbed the eyeliner.

"What did you do?" Abel asked, petting Tiny when the large cat jumped up on the window seat.

"I left. I stopped all communication with him. Fuck, I moved across the country to a tiny town in Maine."

"How did he take it?"

"I got e-mail after e-mail at first. He was confused, then mad. I only sent him one e-mail, telling him that I would always care for him, but that I couldn't be around him or talk to him. It was hard, to not reply to his e-mails and texts, but I did it."

"But you haven't found love," Abel said sadly.

"I don't know if I ever will. Sometimes, I think you only get one soulmate in life."

"That can't be true," Grey said. "There has to be someone out there for you. Abel and I will find him. You'll see."

"Dear god, I think you just became a member of the Hot Mess Club," Abel said.

"Well, it's a good thing your makeup's done," David said. "That means I can run."

He packed up his makeup as Grey ran to the mirror, eager to see the finished product. Damn, he looked good. David had put just the right amount of makeup in just the right places to enhance Grey's features. He looked sexy. "I love you, David."

He laughed and gave Grey a hug. "I love you too, doll face. Now get dressed. You have exactly thirty minutes." He picked up his box and left the room.

"We have to find his new soulmate," Abel said.

"Agreed."

"First, though, you need to get your ass married."

"You're so romantic, Abel," Justin said, closing the door behind him and Caden.

"You only have thirty minutes, Grey," Caden said, picking up the black maternity slacks and the pretty cream shirt. "Get moving."

"Yes, sir," Grey said, saluting. His three friends helped him dress, and he looked at himself in the mirror. "I am one sexy, pregnant man." He felt good, confident, and loved.

A woman poked her head in the door. "I'm so sorry to interrupt, but I'm looking for Grey."

"Georgia?" He had never met her, but he recognized her voice. "Oh my god, what are you doing here?"

The redhead grinned, rushing over to hug him. "It's so good to finally meet you in person. Mr. Delwick and his family are here too. Your father-in-law-to-be invited us all."

"This is so wonderful," he said. "I'm so happy to see you." He introduced her to his friends.

"You're one of the Bensons from Benson and Sons," Georgia said to Caden. "My nephew just graduated law school and applied with you all and a ton of other firms. He's an omega, so most of the other firms sent back a polite, *no, thank you*. He has an interview with your firm though."

"I think I remember Cain talking about it. Your nephew has a lot of potential, and my dad's firm prides itself on fighting inequality. If he doesn't completely screw up the interview, he'll likely be hired."

She clapped happily. "You have no idea how good that is to hear."

Ines opened the door. "Mi corazón, your boss is a wonderful man. I just met him and his husband," she said, then stopped, tearing up. "You look so beautiful."

"Is it time, Abuela?"

"Yes, it is."

"We'll go sit," Caden said. He hugged Grey. Abel, Justin, and Georgia took their turns, and then he was about to get married.

"Abuela, do you think my parents would be happy for me?"

"I have no doubt that they would be happy for you and so damn proud of you. You are a good, sweet boy. Your boss was singing your praises, and Barry showed him the website you've put together for Farm Fresh. He was very impressed. You are so talented and so kind. Look at all your friends and your pets. You have such a big heart, querida. Now, let's get you married."

Johnny Cash's voice filled the room, and "You are my Sunshine" started playing. Grey and his abuela started down the stairs, all eyes on them. All the Wilsons were there, along with the Hot Mess Club and some of Harper's close friends. David sniffled, dabbing at his eyes. Georgia sat between him and a man that could only be Mr. Delwick. The older man smiled widely and nodded, his arm around the older omega beside him. Their four children sat in a row, looking around curiously.

His eyes passed over them all quickly and landed on his sweet alpha. Harper stood nervously at the arbor. Grey grinned. His man had nothing to worry about. Nothing would take his sunshine from him. Absolutely nothing.

The officiate cleared his throat and started the ceremony. Grey barely heard anything at all, but somehow said "I do" at the right time. An eternity later, they turned toward their friends and family.

"I present to you, Greyson and Harper Wilson."

arper helped Grey up into the newly finished sled. He'd rushed, but managed to get it finished in time for the festival. It warmed his heart to have Grey have the first ride in it. Dumpling and Boon were hitched up and decorated with white, green, and gold flowers and ribbons. They shook their heads, demanding attention.

"Good boys," he told them. "Go gentle for our Grey now, okay?"

Gramps tucked the warm, fur-lined blanket around Grey's legs and reached up, kissing his cheek. "You boys be careful on the drive. We'll meet you at the festival."

Shawn hopped in, grabbing the reins, and Harper took a seat beside his husband, sharing his blanket. He wrapped his arms around his omega, and Grey leaned his head against his chest.

"I love you," Grey whispered, eyes a bit dazed. "I can't believe we're married."

"I know, sunshine," Harper said. "If feels like I've been waiting on this for years. Waiting on you."

"No more waiting," Grey said, nuzzling his chest. The sled took off, and their friends and family cheered and tossed dried rosemary their way. His papa said it symbolized love. At least, it smelled good.

"I know I'm from Florida, but I think I love the winters in Maine."

Harper gave his omega a sharp look. "Are you crazy? No one likes the winters in Maine."

"I get snow kisses from you," Grey said, leaning up and kissing him gently. Light snowflakes fell on their heated faces. Grey settled his head back on Harper's chest. "The woods are beautiful and quiet, and I have you here to keep me warm. Maine winters are the best."

They kissed some more, keeping themselves warm, and eventually arrived at the festival. There were already a ton of people there, and Harper helped Grey out of the sled, giving up the ride for another couple. Shawn would spend the next two hours driving couples around. In the cold. While they made out. Harper sent him a sympathetic look, but his brother looked pitiful.

Mr. Delwick and his family were already having fun on the ice rink. He waved cheerfully when he saw them pass, then hurriedly grabbed his toddling omega. The rest of the family spread out, working at stalls or enjoying themselves.

"It must have taken forever to put up this many lights and decorations," Grey said. "I can't believe Papa wanted to have the wedding the same day. Imagine all the work they had to do."

"I feel bad saying this, but I'm really glad I didn't have to help," Harper said, grinning. "Gramps kept telling me that a man shouldn't work on his wedding day."

"Hmm." Grey raised his brow. "That's why you married me, isn't it? To get out of working."

"That's it," Harper said, shrugging. "The fact that you're sweet, loving, kind, silly, and sexy had nothing to do with it. Neither did the fact that I love you. Nothing at all."

Grey snorted. "What do you want to do? I've never really been to a winter festival like this."

"Santa is set up in the middle for all the kids to get pictures with. Don't tell anyone, but it's really Uncle Barry's alpha, Uncle Jamie. Zoe has a couple of booths set up selling baked goods and hot chocolate. There's a ton of coffee carts around here too, but you can't have any of that. Mrs. Bethel has a couple booths selling food. There's one selling lobster mac and cheese and clam chowder. I think the other has Shepard's pie and meat pies. Then they have the ice rink, which you can't do. There's also an ice sculpture contest and a snowman building contest."

"Let's get lobster mac and cheese, then go build a snowwoman," Grey said, bouncing in place. "I love this!"

Grey moaned over the lobster mac and cheese, making Harper's pants distinctly uncomfortable, and the snowman contest got lively.

"Are you sure you want to partner with your boss and my little sister? On our wedding day?" Harper tried to frown, but it must not have come out right. Grey didn't look a bit worried.

"Are you afraid, my sweet alpha?" Grey wore his game face.

"Afraid? Only of you crying all night because Ray and I win."

"Big words, Harper," Zoe said, stretching. "Olive and I will leave you both in the dust, err, snow."

"Children," David said. He shook his head. "Come on, Georgia. Let's show them who's the best."

Mr. Delwick's family and Ines cheered from the sidelines.

"You can do it, my lovely boy," Ines said.

"Kick their butt, honey," Mr. Delwick's omega shouted. Their kids groaned but clapped.

"What's our game plan? Grey, since it's your wedding day, it's only fair you choose," Hannah said.

"Yes," Mr. Delwick said, rubbing his hands together. "You direct, and we'll roll the snow."

"Lead us, oh great one," Hannah added.

"I want to make something magnificent. Something to commemorate this day and my sweet husband," Grey said.

"You're going down, sunshine," Grey's sweet husband hollered. "Ray just came up with a genius idea. I'll still love you even if you lose, okay?"

"Yes," Mr. Delwick said, brow raised. "Let's honor that sweet man."

Grey closed his eyes and took a deep breath.

"Follow my directions, exactly."

~

THIRTY MINUTES LATER, Harper heard Grey say, "This wasn't exactly my vision, but I have to admit it's even better."

"We do what we can," Mr. Delwick said, and Harper looked over to see him bumping fists with Hannah. "Shall we name it?"

"I think this will do," Hannah said, putting the sign beside it. It read *My Sweet Alpha Husband*.

Juan and Carter walked by, pausing to admire their work of art. "Hey, Harper," Juan said. "Your husband's group modeled their snowman on you."

Harper looked up from his and Ray's snowman. It was screaming as it was attacked by several mini snowmen. "Is it perfection in snow form?"

"Yeah," Carter answered. "But it has three boobs."

"They're well-proportioned though. Double Ds," Juan said.

Harper turned all the way around, staring at Grey's snowman. "Why do I have three boobs, sunshine?"

"I'm sorry, but art happens, Harper," Grey said.

"My ass looks good," Harper said, nodding in approval.

"Ugh," Hannah said. "Now all I can see is your ass. Thanks a lot."

"Contestants," Mrs. Webber and Mrs. Bethel said together. "The judging begins."

While Grey's snowman was perfect, the judges

didn't quite agree. Harper knew the truth. Some art was just too complex, or in Harper and Ray's case, too scary. David and Georgia's snowman was a stylish snowwoman. She won second place. First place went to Zoe and Olive's classic snowman with the top hat, carrot nose, and scarf. They'd played it safe.

Zoe and Olive walked past, waving their ribbon. "Bye guys," Zoe said. "First place winners get free hot cocoa."

Olive stopped, eyes widening at Grey's snowman. Mr. Delwick's kids admired it too. "That's the best snowman in the whole world, Uncle Grey," Olive said. "I like his mullet."

"Thanks, sweetheart," Grey said. "Enjoy your cocoa."

"I think we'll join you," Mr. Delwick said, herding his children toward the cocoa booth. He winked at Grey and Hannah. "I had fun you two. Come on, Hannah. I'll buy you a cup."

Harper noticed Grey was drooping. "Let's go sit down," Harper said. "There's a nice bench over there near the woods. It'll be quiet."

"That's perfect," Grey agreed, walking slowly. He heaved a sigh as he sat. "I can't wait until he comes. I want my body back."

A flash of light caught Harper's eye, but it took him a minute to figure out what it was. A man stood in the woods, rifle trained straight toward them. "Grey, get down now!" Harper said, pulling his omega from the bench.

They hit the snow just as the first bullet hit the

bench. Harper curled around Grey, hearing screams and the ping of bullets hitting the bench. Pain seared across his arm, but he ignored it. It was harder to ignore the pain in his shoulder, then his leg. He squeezed Grey to him. His son and his omega were all that mattered.

"Put the gun down," Tanner yelled, standing behind a tree near the shooter. The man ignored him, aiming straight for Grey and Harper. Before he got another shot off, Parker fired from behind another tree, hitting the man in the shoulder. The stranger dropped, crying out, and Tanner rushed forward.

"Harper, Grey," Bennett's voice was shaky. "Boys, are you okay?"

"He's bleeding, Papa," Grey said, sobbing.

Harper looked at his arm. Blood trickled down his arm, dripping onto Grey's stomach. Ouch. "I think the bullet just grazed me," Harper said. "Don't worry, sunshine."

"Your leg and shoulder got hit too," Grey said.

Juan and Carter helped him up, setting him out on the bench. "You'll need to get to the hospital, fast," Juan said. The two men pressed onto his wounds, stifling the bleeding as best they could. Bennett stroked his hair, murmuring comforting words.

"I already called them," Marco said, helping Grey stand.

"Are you okay, Grey?" His omega looked rough.

"I think my water broke," he said, voice cracking. "Harper, you're hurt. I don't like it when you're hurt."

"It'll be okay, sunshine," he said. Spots filled his

vision. "Papa, you'll go with Grey, right? Be there for the baby?"

"I'll take care of him, baby boy," Bennett said, voice fading as Harper passed out.

~

GREY LAY on the hospital bed, contractions coming fast. "Breathe deep, mi corazón," Ines said, holding his hand.

"It'll be over soon, sweetheart," Bennett added, holding his other hand.

"Harper," Grey said, words turning to a screech of pain. Once it faded a bit, he panted. "How's Harper?"

Marco popped his head in. "He's having surgery now, son. Don't you worry a bit. I know my boy, and he'll pull through this." He darted back out to the seating area to wait for news.

"Abuela," he said. "It hurts." He hated whining, but he couldn't help it. He needed massive amounts of doughnuts, hugs, and fucking coffee. He needed his alpha.

"I wish I could take this pain from you, querido," she said.

"I want Harper," he said, crying. They were going to do this together. He'd promised.

"He wants to be here too, sweetheart," Bennett said, stroking his head.

"He can't die," Grey said. "We can't lose him."

"You won't," Ines said. "I know it, my darling boy. I know it. Today is just the day everything wanted to happen. Tomorrow will be better."

He screamed again, and the doctor came in, suited up. He poked around, being as gentle as he could. "You're doing great, Mr. Wilson," he said. "Before you know it, you'll be holding your baby boy."

A little less than ten hours later, Rue Bishop Wilson was settled onto his papa's chest. Ines and Bennett both cried. Grey looked at his son. He was so beautiful. The most beautiful thing Grey had ever seen. His dark brown skin was freshly washed and so soft. Rue had Grey's silky brown hair, blond shoots already visible. Grey had already counted his toes and fingers and noted his little omega line. Now, he was wrapped tightly in his small, jersey-patterned swaddle sack.

Bennett pulled out his phone and took a ton of pictures, tears falling down his cheeks. "You made a beautiful baby, Grey."

"Have you heard about Harper," he asked. "Is he okay?"

"I'll go find Marco," Ines said. "I need to let them know Rue is here anyway. You just rest, bebé." She kissed his head and left.

"Here's his first bottle," a nurse said, handing it to Grey. She showed him how to hold Rue, then left them to it. His son took a little time to figure out the nipple. Bennett and Grey shared some giggles but cheered softly when he started drinking.

Ines and Marco came in, wearing grins. "Harper is just fine, querido," Ines said. "All the bullets were removed. His leg needed some extra work, because an artery was hit. The doctors say he'll be fine with time. As soon as he wakes up, we'll let you know."

Grey tried to stifle his sobs, but he couldn't. Marco picked up Rue, continuing to feed him and Bennett wrapped his arms around Grey. The older man cried with him. Grey wasn't upset; he was exhausted. His alpha was alright, his baby was born, and he was tired. So damn tired. This morning had been all about excitement and love. Now, it was just relief.

"The shooter was identified as Gerald Lane. The truck he tried to run you over with was in the parking lot. He'll live, but he'll do some time. Caden is already putting together a civil lawsuit," Marco said. "He'll pay for what he did, Grey. I promise."

"Caden can't be our lawyer," Grey said.

"Why not?" Bennett wiped his eyes and sat up.

"I can't say, but he doesn't want to."

"I really, really do want to be your lawyer," Caden said from the door. Abel and Justin stood on either side of him. The Hot Mess Club was here. "This is different, so I'm fine with it."

"Are you sure?" Grey watched closely as Marco passed little Rue over to Abel. He cooed to Grey's son, rocking him gently.

"I'm sure. Now let me hold that baby," Caden said. Abel reluctantly handed him over.

His friends and family slowly came in and out of the room to see the baby. A very distraught Mr. Delwick stopped by to check on him and the baby. He didn't say much, but Grey had a feeling there was a conversation there. Grey closed his eyes for just a moment. He wanted to watch Rue, to hear about Harper, but he was so damn tired.

CHAPTER 16

Christmas day dawned clear and white. Grey rocked Rue, feeding him a bottle, and watched Harper sleep, Tiny curled up next to him. They were home, finally, but Harper was on bedrest for at least another week. His alpha's eyes fluttered open, and he smiled at the sight of Grey and Rue.

He deftly sat up, holding out his good arm. "Let me hold him. Please?"

Grey smiled and gently handed Rue to his daddy. Grey had cried when Harper first laid eyes on the baby. Harper had been speechless, eyes full of wonder. His sweet alpha had fallen in love, completely and irrevocably. Now, if Harper was awake, he wanted his little boy with him. Grey laughed as Tiny sniffed Rue and then decided to ignore them, falling back asleep.

He bent and picked up Butterball and Opal. If he couldn't hold his human baby, he'd hold his animal babies. Chewy poked Grey's back with his nose, reminding him of his big baby. He leaned down and kissed his fuzzy head. "We have so many little ones," Grey said. "At least Opal is potty-trained now."

"I'm a good teacher," Hannah said, walking in the room with a breakfast tray for Harper. "I just finished with the ponies and the chickens, Harper." She was staying with them over Christmas break to help, but Bennett and Marco came over everyday and someone usually stayed the night too. They had plenty of help, which let Harper relax and heal. Gramps was even working daily in Harper's workshop, helping him stay on schedule with his commissioned pieces. Having a family was something special.

"Will you two be alright while I'm gone?" Grey asked.

"We'll be fine," Hannah said. "Papa is downstairs and will hog the baby when Harper falls asleep. You've already fed these guys and pampered your rabbits."

"You're a life saver, Hannah, you know that?" Harper looked up from staring adoringly at Rue. "Thanks."

The girl rolled her eyes. "You guys are family. What else would I do? Oh, and don't forget Caden's present. She's downstairs now. I just took her to visit her beloved."

Grey smiled. "Perfect. I'll see you all in a few hours." He bent to kiss Harper, then dropped a soft kiss on Rue's forehead. The baby scrunched up his face, making Grey laugh. He headed for the door, then paused to hug Hannah. "You really are the best."

She held onto him longer than he expected. "Can I talk to you a minute?"

"Sure, Hany," he said and pulled her into the hallway. "What's wrong?"

Hannah nibbled her lip, looking unusually hesitant. "I met someone at school. I really like them."

"That's great! Why are you worried? Do they not like you? If that's the case, then they're an idiot."

"It's a girl. Her name's Summer."

"Is she nice? What's she like?"

"You don't mind that I like girls?"

Grey's mouth dropped open. What. The. Hell. "Are you kidding me? Hany, we love you so damn much. Nothing would ever change that. Plus, there's nothing wrong with liking girls instead of boys. How many gay men are in our family anyway?"

"A lot," she said with a smile. "It's just that all the girls in the family like boys too. I'm different."

"You're different alright, but every single one of us is different. You are *you,* which is a very special person. No one will be mad or disappointed in you, Hany, as long as you're honest."

"You really think so?" She looked relieved, and Grey wanted to kick himself for not noticing that she was so worried.

"I absolutely know so."

"Summer's parents kicked her out when she told them she liked girls. She went to live with her brother, and his wife told him that either Summer had to go or she would."

"That poor girl," Grey said. "What happened?"

"Her brother got a divorce and full custody of his son. They just moved here."

"Good on them," Grey said. "You know your family will never give you up. They'll haunt you forever, whether you like it or not."

She hugged him tightly, then ran back into the bedroom to supervise Harper and Rue. Grey stopped to hug Bennett and make sure he was drinking his tea. The poor man had been hit hard with morning sickness the last few days.

"Don't forgot your bag," Bennett said, nodding to the kitchen chair.

Grey grabbed it and the leash for Caden's present. The small dog was a mutt. She was white, with thick curly hair, ears that dragged on the ground, and a long body. Her tail was one big curl. She was sweet and loving, just what Caden needed.

"Come on, cutie. Time to meet your new best friend." Grey put the dog and his bag in the car, then drove closer to the barn. It would be hard, but the little dog had bonded with Huckleberry, one of Grey's Angora rabbits. Grey had a carrier all set up and put the huge black and grey rabbit in it. Caden would be getting two presents.

A short, scary, sliding drive later, Grey arrived at the Bensons' vacation lake home. Caden had been staying there for the few weeks he'd been in town, and the rest of his family had arrived late last night. Abel and Justin sat on the porch with Caden, and Grey saw a lovely older woman peek out the window several times as he walked from his car, juggling the carrier and the leash.

"Did you guys get another dog," Justin asked. "Is that really a good idea? You have a baby now."

"This isn't my dog," he said, shrugging. "Merry Christmas, Caden," he said, handing over the little dog's leash.

Caden stared at him blankly, slowly reaching out to take the leash. "You got me a dog?"

"Yes," Grey said excitedly. "She's two years old and a mixed breed doggy. She's had all her shots and is fixed."

"Aww," Abel said. "She's the perfect little writer's dog." He scratched her ears and watched her little tail wag.

"She also comes with Huckleberry here. He's her one true love, and, like most of the bunnies in my collection, he's litter box trained. Lucky you, right?" He set the crate in front of Caden's feet.

Justin laughed loudly. "Lucky Caden," he wheezed when he could.

Grey kicked him gently in the shin. "You and Tanner are getting a baby bunny in a few weeks as a late Christmas present, so I wouldn't laugh too hard. You'll have to potty train her yourself." Juliet had given birth to six babies the same day Grey had Rue. Between Grey and Hannah, they would be weaned soon.

Abel shook his head. "Are you ready to do this, Caden? Your mother has peeked outside a hundred times since we got here."

Caden sighed. "We'd better." He picked up the crate and led his new dog to the door.

His mother opened it as soon as he stepped in front of it. "Caden, darling, are you going to come inside and introduce us to your friends?" Susan Benson was a beautiful woman, but worry creased her brow.

"Yes, Mom," Caden said, waving them inside. The large cabin was immaculate and finely decorated. Two men stood when they marched in. The older man looked just like an older version of Carter. Grey thought he must be John. The younger man was sharp. He didn't seem surprised to see them, and Grey wondered if Caden had already confided in his brother.

"These are my friends, Grey and Justin. I'm sure you remember Abel. Guys, this is Cain, John, and Susan."

"Who is this little girl?" Susan asked, bending to pet Caden's new friend.

"She is my Christmas present from Grey. I haven't named her yet. This is apparently Huckleberry, another present." Caden held up the carrier, staring at the large Angora rabbit. "Should I let him out?"

"He'd appreciate it. Just leave his cage open so he can get to the litter box," Grey said.

Caden did as he said, and Huckleberry hopped out, going straight to his dog friend.

"While it's nice to meet your friends, son, you've been on edge all morning. What's wrong? Why did you insist on sitting on the porch until your friends got here?" John looked as worried as his wife.

Caden took a deep breath, and Grey linked his arm with the alpha's while Justin did the same on his other side. Abel stood on Grey's other side in solidarity. "I have something important to tell you, and they insisted on being here for moral support," Caden said.

"Son, you can tell us anything. I thought we'd worked this out with Carter's situation," Susan said.

"I'm quitting the law firm," Caden said bluntly. His father's eyes widened in disbelief, and Susan's knees buckled. She fell gracefully into her seat.

"You're branching off on your own? Why? Do you want to move out of Georgia?" John fell into his own seat.

"I won't be practicing law formally," Caden said. "I enjoy helping family when I can, so I won't stop practicing all together, but I'm changing professions and moving to Hobson Hills."

"Oh, Caden," Susan said. "Did we push you into it like we tried to do with Carter?"

Caden clammed up.

Grey knew he dreaded hurting his family, but they needed to understand. "Um, you kind of did," Grey said. "He really loves and respects you, so he naturally wanted to please you both." He rubbed Caden's arm.

"Is that true, son?" John looked devastated.

"Yes, but it's not your fault," Caden said. "I could have said no, but I didn't know what I wanted, and it was far easier to go into law. I didn't realize that I would grow to hate it so much."

"Gramps already found him a nice little cabin a mile down the road. It's on the lake too," Abel said.

"We can promote Smithson to his place," Cain said. "The transition won't be a problem at all."

"What about you, Cain? Do you hate law too? I don't want you boys to be unhappy," John said.

"I happen to love law, so don't worry about it. I may

have been steered that way too, but it turned out well for me," Cain said. "Caden will find his own path and be just as happy as Carter and I are."

"Anything you need, Caden, please let me know. Do you have another profession in mind? It's never too late to start again," John said.

"I'm a writer. I've had a contract with a publisher for three years now," Caden said. "I write under the pen name, Roxanne Baxter."

Susan squealed in a very un-ladylike manner. "I love that author. That's you? Oh, you're so talented, Caden." She hugged him tightly, dislodging Grey and Justin who were laughing.

"So you're well-known," John asked hesitantly.

"He is, darling," Susan said. "He was on the *New York Times* bestseller list at least three times that I recall. He is a wonderful romance author."

"Romance?" Cain grinned. "You write romance novels?"

"Very successful ones," Abel said, hands on his hips. "There's absolutely nothing wrong with an alpha writing romance novels."

"It shows how well-rounded he is. The omegas are going to love him," Justin said.

John grinned. "My son, the romance novelist." He shook his head. "I'm so glad you finally told us, Caden. We're proud of you."

A small smile graced Caden's face. "Thank you, Dad."

Grey tackled the alpha in a hug. His friend would be okay.

CHAPTER 17

"Merry Christmas, Mr. Delwick," Grey said happily. He finished stuffing Butterball into her new Christmas outfit. She wasn't pleased, but she looked cute.

"Merry Christmas to you too, Grey," his boss said. "I wanted to check up on you and your husband. I can't apologize enough for what Lane did."

"Again, Mr. Delwick," Grey said firmly, "it was Lane's fault. It was his decision to steal other people's work. It was his decision to try to hurt me and Harper. You had no part in his decisions."

The older alpha sighed. "I know you're right, but I still feel guilty. We were having such fun, and you were so happy."

"Here I am, Christmas day, happy and having fun," Grey said. "It'll be alright. Does your husband still plan on coming for a visit in the summer? Gramps and Grammy are already planning activities. I think they like your husband more than their own children."

Mr. Delwick laughed. "You have a wonderful family, Grey, and we will certainly be up in the summer. You have a great day, and tell your husband I said hello."

"I will," Grey promised, running into the kitchen and kissing Bennett's cheek. He stole a cookie, then darted back out, running to answer the door, cheeks full of gooey yumminess.

HARPER AND OPAL relaxed in Grey's comfy chair in front of the fire, Harper's injured leg propped up on a pillow on the ottoman. All the Wilsons and Bensons were gathered in the house for their usual early Christmas dinner. They always left the mornings to the individual families, but around two, they all gathered together to exchange gifts and eat a delicious ham dinner.

This year, Grammy and Gramps insisted that it would be at Harper and Grey's house instead of theirs. Little Rue didn't need to be out in the snow, and Harper was supposed to be on bedrest. His house was packed, but he wouldn't have had it any other way. His omega darted around, talking and laughing with David. Chewy followed the two men faithfully.

The Bensons, Juan, and Ray all mixed in, perfectly at ease with the Wilsons. Olive's best friend, Shelly, and her family were there as well. They were becoming a part of the Wilson clan all on their own. Surprisingly, Tanner, Justin, and Justin's mom were there too.

Tanner and Justin fit right in, but Justin's mom had been hesitant until Grammy had taken the fragile woman under her wing.

Caden carried his dog over and set him down on Harper's lap. Opal protested, but then settled back down, happy to sniff the new dog. "Will you watch Sassy? Shawn and I are handing out the presents."

"Sure," he said, petting Sassy's long ears. Her sweet black eyes watched him as her tongue lolled from her mouth. "She doesn't seem very high maintenance."

"She is the sweetest animal I've ever met. Huckleberry is the second sweetest, but Olive and the other kids have him," Caden said. He gave Sassy a pat, then went in search of Shawn.

"How's my sweet alpha?" Grey said, arms wrapping around Harper from behind the chair. "You doing alright?"

"I'm good," he said, yawning. "I miss my baby boy though." He pouted.

"Abuela is showing him off. He's wearing his Captain America bodysuit and the striped pants. He's so adorable."

"What's Butterball wearing?" Harper said, knowing his omega enjoyed dressing the poor pets up.

"I put her in her pretty red tutu," he said, face lit with joy. "Chewy here refused to wear his sweater." Grey hugged Chewy and kissed his ear.

Harper shared a look with the large dog. Yeah, Chewy was the smart one. Hmm, maybe Tiny was actually the smartest. The large Maine Coon always headed for the bedroom when they had company.

"Present time, everyone," Anna said. "Gather in the living room. Shawn and Caden are Santa's helpers this year."

Presents were passed out, and the present frenzy began. Lucky Harper got two more knitted scarves and a very lopsided beanie from Grey. The pets also received their new knitted goods.

"Gramps," Grey wailed, holding up the new, and larger, recipe box. "I love it." He rushed to Harper's grandfather and hugged the man.

"Grey, why did you give us each a picture of you holding a baby rabbit?" Abel asked. "Justin, Abuela, David, Janelle, Zoe, and I all got one."

"Read the back," Grey said, still hugging Gramps. "You're becoming a bunny daddy in a few weeks." Good-natured groans greeted his words, but Harper knew they'd all love the rabbits and take good care of them.

Ernie cheered. "Give all their hair to me, guys."

Harper gave Shawn a nod, and his brother whispered to Grey. It was time for Harper's Christmas present to Grey.

GREY FOLLOWED SHAWN OUTSIDE. It was late afternoon, but the sun was sinking fast. Shawn looked back over his shoulder, smiling shyly. "I know we haven't spent a lot of time together, but Harper explained about your brother."

Shame filled Grey. He *had* avoided Shawn as much

as he could. The young man reminded him so much of Rue and was almost the same age as his brother when he died. "I'm sorry, Shawn. I've been making progress, but not enough. I'll get better."

"You'll get there when you get there. I'll be waiting on you," he said, holding the crook of his arm out for Grey to hold.

Grey took it, noticing they were going to the edge of the forest near the fenced pasture. There was a solid, weathered bench right at the edge of the woods. Grey had never noticed it before. Shawn had him sit, then sat beside him.

"Harper wanted to share this with you, but he can't come outside. He wanted to show you his Christmas gift for you."

"What did he do?" Grey looked around, but didn't see anything.

"This is the spot where he's going to help you plant three winterberry bushes, each mixed with the ashes of your family. The ashes will help the bushes grow, and you'll have a spot to visit them, honoring their memory."

Grey covered his mouth, eyes watering. He could see the three colorful bushes set against the dark bareness of the forest. The bright red berries would stand out, a spot of color against the light and darkness. He started to cry in earnest, and Shawn wrapped his arms around him.

"We'll do it in the spring," Shawn said, his voice cracking. "The berries will give birds, raccoon, mice, and other animals food in the winter."

"Thank you, Shawn, for doing this," Grey said, trying to stop his tears.

"It's no problem. I can't imagine losing my Dad, Papa, Hannah, and Harper. I wish you still had your parents and your brother, but I know that's the past and it can't be changed. We're here for you though. We won't take their places, but we'll mourn with you and hold you. You aren't alone anymore, Grey. You're a Wilson."

LATER THAT NIGHT, long after everyone left, Grey curled up with his sweet alpha. His head rested on Harper's good shoulder, and he watched his beautiful husband sleep. A month ago, he had gone to bed alone, Rue in his belly, afraid and worried for the future. He'd thought he'd lose his best friend and his Abuela.

Tonight, he'd fall asleep next to his alpha. He would get up a few times to feed Rue and cuddle his adorable son. Tomorrow, he would go visit his Abuela in town and have lunch with his friends and family.

Life was truly beautiful.

OTHER BOOKS BY C.W. GRAY

The Blue Solace Series – science fiction/fantasy, gay
romance, mpreg

1. The Mercenary's Mate
2. The General's Mate
3. The Soldier's Mate
4. The Lieutenant's Mate
5. The Engineer's Mate
6. The Captain's Mate

The Hobson Hills Omegas – non-shifter, gay romance,
mpreg, omegaverse

1. Falling for the Omega
2. Snow Kisses for My Omega
3. Romancing the Omega
4. Healing the Omega
5. A Pint for my Omega
6. Unraveling the Omega
7. The Alpha's Christmas Wish

Hobson Hills Shorts – short stories from the world of
Hobson Hills Omegas

1. The Beta's Love Song
2. Bennett's Dream
3. Justin's Journey

4. Grey's Gift

The Silver Isles – paranormal, merman, gay romance, mpreg, paranormal

1. The Guppy Prince – *Coming Soon*
2. The Not so Little Merman – *Coming Soon*
3. The Sea Witch – *Coming Soon*

If you would like to keep up with releases, please like and follow me on Facebook at @cwgrayauthor, visit my website at https://cwgray-author.com, or join C.W. Gray's Reading Nook on Facebook.

www.ingramcontent.com/pod-product-compliance
Lightning Source LLC
Chambersburg PA
CBHW050539190726
48284CB00003B/1139